W9-BAO-462

"You're scaring me,"

Dawn said, aware that she was taking the easy way out in blaming him. She didn't know whether to blame her own longings, or the intensity of being together in the dark like this. And what scared her most were the feelings he aroused.

"I don't mean to scare you." He leaned closer, her hand securely enclosed in his. "Don't fight whatever it is you're feeling, Dawn. Share it with me."

"There's nothing to share," she said emphatically, trying to convince herself as well as him. "This room is giving me the creeps—that's all!"

"Go to bed."

"No!"

"I'm afraid..." He paused. His face was so close to hers, his breath tickled her chin.

"Not you?"

"I'm afraid I'm going to kiss you again."

Dear Reader,

This month, our FABULOUS FATHER starts off Linda Varner's exciting new series, MR. RIGHT, INC. The trilogy features three pals who find love at first site—construction site that is. Ethan Cooper is a *Dad on the Job*. He wasn't looking for love—just a good life for him and his kids. Then he met Nicole Winter....

Favorite author Marie Ferrarella continues her BABY'S CHOICE series with *Baby Times Two*. In this heartwarming series, matchmaking babies bring together their unsuspecting parents—and inspire them to love.

Silhouette Romance is proud to present the newest star to the line, Christie Clark. Her book, *Two Hearts Too Late*, is our PREMIERE title. We know you'll be pleased with this emotional story of two people who fall in love—in the midst of a custody battle.

Wedding bells are ringing for two of our couples this month. Watch Kristi Beeler turn handsome cynic Matt Stewart into a dashing groom in Maris Soule's *Stop the Wedding!* And Ben Danvers and Chelsea Carson strike a marriage bargain in Donna Clayton's latest book, *Wife for a While*.

What happens when a handsome ghost hunter and a beautiful skeptic join forces to investigate the strange happenings in an old house? Find out in *Turn Back the Night* by Jennifer Drew—an exciting SPELLBOUND title.

I hope you've enjoyed Silhouette Romance this month. In the coming months look for books by Elizabeth August, Helen R. Myers, Joleen Daniels, Carla Cassidy and many more of your favorite authors!

Happy reading!

Anne Canadeo
Senior Editor

Please address questions and book requests to:
Silhouette Reader Service
U.S.: 3010 Walden Ave., P.O. Box 1325, Buffalo, NY 14269
Canadian: P.O. Box 609, Fort Erie, Ont. L2A 5X3

TURN BACK THE NIGHT

Jennifer Drew

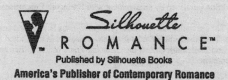

Silhouette

R O M A N C E™

Published by Silhouette Books

America's Publisher of Contemporary Romance

If you purchased this book without a cover you should be aware
that this book is stolen property. It was reported as "unsold and
destroyed" to the publisher, and neither the author nor the
publisher has received any payment for this "stripped book."

To Erik, Ari and Matt

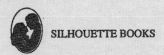

SILHOUETTE BOOKS

ISBN 0-373-19040-9

TURN BACK THE NIGHT

Copyright © 1994 by Pamela Hanson & Barbara Andrews

All rights reserved. Except for use in any review, the reproduction
or utilization of this work in whole or in part in any form by any
electronic, mechanical or other means, now known or hereafter
invented, including xerography, photocopying and recording, or in
any information storage or retrieval system, is forbidden without
the written permission of the editorial office, Silhouette Books,
300 East 42nd Street, New York, NY 10017 U.S.A.

All characters in this book have no existence outside the imagination of
the author and have no relation whatsoever to anyone bearing the same
name or names. They are not even distantly inspired by any individual
known or unknown to the author, and all incidents are pure invention.

This edition published by arrangement with Harlequin Enterprises B. V.

® and TM are trademarks of Harlequin Enterprises B. V., used under
license. Trademarks indicated with ® are registered in the United States
Patent and Trademark Office, the Canadian Trade Marks Office and in
other countries.

Printed in U.S.A.

JENNIFER DREW

is a mother-daughter writing team who live in Wisconsin and West Virginia, respectively. Before they became partners, Mom, a columnist for an antique newspaper, was the author of twenty-one category romances and her daughter was a journalist and teacher. Both are thrilled to be writing together.

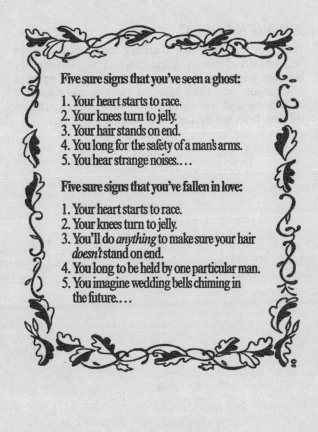

Five sure signs that you've seen a ghost:

1. Your heart starts to race.
2. Your knees turn to jelly.
3. Your hair stands on end.
4. You long for the safety of a man's arms.
5. You hear strange noises....

Five sure signs that you've fallen in love:

1. Your heart starts to race.
2. Your knees turn to jelly.
3. You'll do *anything* to make sure your hair *doesn't* stand on end.
4. You long to be held by one particular man.
5. You imagine wedding bells chiming in the future....

Chapter One

Dawn turned onto the unpaved country road expecting to see a spooky Victorian mansion, the kind that belonged on the cover of a Gothic novel. Instead she found a charming house set among towering pines and oaks.

Her sister's recently purchased home was old but pretty, a country residence with doves and hearts cut out of the shiny black shutters. It was a two-story house built early in the century when people were tired of gingerbread and turrets. The design was classic Americana, a style modern builders were recreating in the northern Chicago suburb where Dawn lived. With narrow wooden siding freshly painted a soft dove gray and trimmed in white, the house certainly didn't look haunted.

Stopping her van at the end of the gravel driveway, Dawn was totally mystified by her sister's fear of the benign-looking house. It wasn't like Linda to be afraid of shadows or to imagine spooky happenings. When she'd called, asking Dawn to come as soon as possible, she'd been reluctant to give details. One thing was certain: Linda was afraid of something, and she didn't want to face it alone.

Since their mother's death nearly five years ago, the sisters had relied on each other. Linda had her husband, of course, but Gary Hall was just building his career, traveling a lot and often gone for extended periods of time. Maybe Linda was lonesome....

Shaking her head in denial, Dawn drove the van closer to the house. Linda might miss Gary a lot, but she wouldn't beg Dawn to visit just to keep her company. Her husband was doing well as an electronics consultant, and Linda had always seemed resigned to his long trips. Now he was in Japan for an indefinite stay, leaving Linda alone in this remote part of central Wisconsin in their recently purchased house.

Dawn stepped down from her Dodge van, glad to stretch after driving more than four hours. Linda had sounded almost hysterical at the beginning of her early morning phone call, but anyone could get a case of the creeps alone in a big house during an early summer storm. Today the sky was a cloudless azure blue and the sun gave an emerald glow to the heavily wooded area outside the small town of Ottawa. On a June day like this, Dawn could understand why a young married couple might be enticed into buying an old house on the fringe of a beautiful pine forest.

Young! She smiled, wondering how old they had to be before she stopped thinking of her twenty-four-year-old sister as a kid. Although she was only four years older, Dawn had felt motherly toward her sibling since their father had deserted them, leaving their mom to cope alone with supporting and raising two school-age daughters.

"Dawn! I'm glad you didn't get lost!"

Taking off her sunglasses, Dawn saw her sister through the screens enclosing the front porch. "Not this time. Your directions were great."

Linda bounded down the wooden steps to the lawn and threw her arms around Dawn. "I shouldn't tease you about your sense of direction. I'm so glad you're here!"

"I was overdue for a visit. Sorry I couldn't get here even sooner. I had to finish a few things before I could get away."

"I know how you hate to leave your business." Linda hugged her again, then locked her arm through Dawn's. "How's the antique mall doing?"

"Not bad." Dawn had one superstition: admitting to success might jinx it. "Every spot is rented for the summer. We have seven new dealers."

"I would never have enough nerve to start a business in such a huge, old factory building."

"Neither would I, if I didn't have Jane as a partner. She's good in everything I'm not."

"There's nothing you can't do!" Linda squeezed her arm so hard, Dawn wondered if her exuberance was partly hysteria. What was happening inside this inviting country residence?

"When will Gary be home?"

"He may have to stay another month, but he's working like a demon to get home sooner. We talked about meeting in Japan, but it's really too expensive for me to fly there. With mortgage payments and all the work we've had done on this place.... Well, come on in! You won't think we're quite so crazy for buying it when you see the inside."

"My bags..."

"We'll get them later. No need to lock the van. People here don't even lock their houses."

"I couldn't sleep with my door unlocked."

"Don't worry. I still shut the place up like a fortress at night. Old habits die hard, but there's nothing outside the house that scares me."

"About that story you told me..."

"Aaron doesn't want me to repeat it again until he gets his recorder working. That way he'll get a fresher version, I guess. He's upstairs now trying some new batteries."

"What are you talking about? Who's Aaron?" Dawn stepped into the cool interior of the porch, noticing an old-fashioned metal glider suspended on chains from the ceiling.

"Aaron Mead. Dr. Aaron Mead. He's with the university in Madison."

"Is he a friend of yours? I've been worried sick ever since you called."

"He's not exactly a friend." Linda opened a door with etched glass panels set into the wall on either side and gestured toward a large entryway with an antique hall stand.

"Who is he, then?" Dawn asked, her concern intensified by her sister's secretive manner.

"Come in, we'll talk about it," Linda promised.

Another door with a full-length panel of glass opened into the living room, and Dawn glanced around with admiration. Wide, golden oak woodwork was set off by plush, deep apricot carpeting. The walls were a paler shade of the same color, and the forest green living room set she'd given Linda as a wedding gift could have been designed especially for this room. An elegant marble fireplace was on the right, and an arched opening on the left led to a less formal room with Gary's desk, a TV, and odds and ends of comfortable furniture randomly arranged.

"It's really nice," Dawn said, impressed by the understated charm of the front rooms.

"It's paradise after living in cramped apartments. Gary refinished all the woodwork down here, plus the hall tree. Every time he gets near a piece of old wood, he wants to start stripping it."

"Linda, I'm dying to know what's going on here!"

"In a minute. I hope calling you to come didn't interrupt anything important."

"No, it's fine. Jane took two weeks of vacation to ski with her husband in February, and she'll feel guilty if I don't take the same amount of time this summer."

She didn't want to make her sister feel guilty by telling her she'd hoped to use her time off to visit a school friend in Virginia and do some heavy auction-buying to restock her booth in the mall. She and Jane were partners in renovating the old building and renting spaces to seventy-two other dealers, but they both had individual setups to sell their own finds.

"I was hoping you could stay awhile. Gary will be gone at least two more weeks. His company is negotiating with a Japanese firm to build components in this country."

"Are you going to look for a job?"

"No. He thinks I have too much to do taking care of the house."

"Linda . . ." Dawn was concerned, as always, by her sister's total dependence on her husband, but she didn't want to start her visit by giving unwanted advice. Linda would always seek male approval—and Dawn would always be grateful she'd had the determination to make it on her own after a broken engagement. "Show me the rest of the house," she suggested.

"We still have a lot to— Aaron, I didn't hear you come down."

A man moved silently through the dining room and the large archway that opened into the front room. He was dressed in ordinary faded jeans and a red knit shirt open at his throat, but Dawn had a fanciful notion that he belonged in pirate garb. His thick hair, worn long enough to curl over his ears, was raven black, and his dark brown eyes seemed to appraise everything he saw, adding to the impression that he should be carrying a cutlass, not a leather-bound notebook and a ballpoint. He had broad shoulders and narrow hips, a build that accentuated the impression that he liked a rugged way of life, and she'd never seen a beard that attracted her so much. As dark as his hair and carefully trimmed, it made her wonder if it would feel as silky as it looked.

"Aaron, this is my sister, Dawn Girard."

He nodded solemnly and offered his hand, but Dawn had the feeling he was secretly amused about something. One black brow was slightly higher than the other, calling attention to his warm, mahogany brown eyes and thick, spiky lashes.

"Dawn, this is Dr. Mead."

"Aaron," he said, grasping her hand with more pressure than was called for.

"You're...?"

"The ghost hunter." He smiled broadly, his firm, expressive lips parting to reveal nearly flawless white teeth.

His friendly smile made her heart flutter a little, but she thought he was almost too handsome for comfort. With high cheekbones and hair swept back from what she thought of as an aristocratic forehead, he intrigued Dawn more than any imaginary ghost. What the devil was he doing in her sister's home?

"Linda told me you were coming. I'm happy to meet you." He finally released her hand, leaving her with a warm sensation spreading to her wrist. "I think the recorder will be all right now. You'll probably be more at ease having your sister here while I record, Linda, so it works out well."

"I don't understand what this is all about," Dawn said.

Aaron saw the puzzled glance she directed at her sister and tried to hide his reaction. He was used to skeptics and curious onlookers overseeing his investigations, but they were seldom so beautiful they made his throat ache. If he'd given it any thought, he would have expected Linda's relative to be attractive. Linda herself was cute enough with a mass of yellow-blond hair and a pert little face that made him feel protective—no doubt she had the same effect on every man she met. Her sister resembled her, but Dawn's beauty was more mature. Her hair was darker than Linda's, a tawny brown with golden glints, and he couldn't be sure if her eyes were hazel or green. She was four or five inches shorter than him, maybe five foot six, but her slender build and square shoulders gave an illusion of greater height. He especially liked her long, graceful neck; her soft, creamy throat was nothing less than elegant.

"You're probably wondering just what I'm doing here," he said, sensing that she liked people to be direct with her. "Let's sit and talk about it."

Her brows came closer together when she frowned, and he wondered what a smile would do to her features.

"Linda is proud of you. You run your own business, I understand," he said, making small talk while he tried to recover from the effect she had on him. He rarely felt so cordial to a person in the first minute they met.

"Yes." He made her feel like straightening her clothes or patting her hair. She couldn't remember the last time she'd felt like squirming because a man seemed to enjoy looking at her.

"She started selling at flea markets and moved up to doing antiques shows," Linda said, speaking for her sister. "Now she and her partner have a big, year-round mall with spaces rented out to other dealers. She even did the design work to renovate the building, an old sausage factory that closed years ago."

"Dr. Mead isn't here to hear about my business," Dawn said, embarrassed by her sister's enthusiasm.

She was soft-spoken, but her voice had a compelling quality that reached him in places below his neck.

She wanted to know a lot more about him. Where on earth had Linda met him? Why hadn't she ever mentioned him before?

"I'm here to investigate what's going on in this house. I'm mostly interested in how people react to the paranormal, but I've made a serious study of psychic phenomena."

"Do you do this for a living?" Dawn had read about people who actually investigated haunted houses, but she'd always harbored the suspicion that fiction writers and tabloid reporters invented them.

"No, only to satisfy my own curiosity. I'm a professor at the University of Wisconsin."

"What field?"

"Psychology."

She looked more puzzled than before but didn't ask another question.

"I did my undergraduate work at UW-Madison and my doctoral work at Northwestern," he said, feeling a bit silly because he was so eager to present his credentials. He'd long ago given up apologizing for his interest in the paranormal or trying to pass it off as a hobby of little importance.

"Interesting," she said, looking more confused than impressed. "But I can't stand the suspense. I'm here because Linda is afraid of something. Please, one of you, tell me what's going on."

"Fair enough." It was, but he had the uncomfortable feeling she wouldn't like his answer. "Linda may have had a paranormal experience."

"Like seeing a ghost—if there were such a thing?"

"Believe it or not, I'm as skeptical as you are. In most cases there's a perfectly rational explanation."

"But not always," Linda said, sounding a little breathless.

"What are you going to do about...whatever?" her sister asked.

She put her questions in a direct, no-nonsense way. He admired her style but wondered whether they were going to be adversaries.

"I ran across a newspaper clipping about a couple in Madison who are renovating a historic home there. They mentioned living with a ghost in their last house."

"In this house! They sold it to us without mentioning the ghost!" Linda said.

"Realtors don't list that kind of information." Dawn tried to joke about it, but she was liking this situation less and less. "What I really want to know is when you contacted my sister."

"About a week ago."

"Before she noticed anything unusual about the house?"

"Yes."

Dawn studied his face, telling herself she only wanted to see his reaction.

"I see your point. You think I planted the idea in Linda's mind."

"I'm only trying to find out what's happening here. Linda's here alone. I worry about her when Gary's gone. I don't like this situation—not at all, Dr. Mead."

"I'm here to help any way I can. There's a possibility you'll experience the same things."

"Dawn, I know what you're thinking—that I'm imagining things because I get lonely when Gary's gone," her sister said.

That was exactly what Dawn suspected, but Linda must need to hear it from someone else—an authority like Dr. Aaron Mead. But from what he said, he wasn't here as a psychologist. He was looking for ghosts or some such nonsense!

"Do you really investigate with an open mind? You're not just writing a book or something?" she asked.

His eyes met hers with disarming directness.

"I'm compiling a file of cases that can't be explained by ordinary means, but publishing a ghost hunter's journal wouldn't do my academic career any good. Just the opposite. I've already paid a high price for my interest in psychic phenomena."

"I can't believe there's anything for you to do here."

"Possibly not, but I'm using my summer break to investigate possible paranormal activities. This house is the most promising so far this year."

Dawn thought of asking more about the price he'd paid for his interest in supernatural things, but she was too concerned about the situation to ask personal questions.

"What you're talking about is just too weird."

This was a problem she didn't know how to handle. She liked to make decisions with concrete objectives, like whether to buy the collection of antique mesh evening bags that had been offered to her, or how to best enforce their new policy banning reproductions in the mall. Why was Linda involving her in something so totally off-the-wall?

"Maybe I'll just be in the way. I really don't think I can go along with something this weird. I have a strong feeling that one of us should leave."

"Oh, Dawn, please stay and give Aaron a chance," her sister pleaded.

Whatever the reason, she couldn't deny one thing: Linda was genuinely afraid. Maybe there was a reason for fear, but the ghost hunter was much more unsettling to Dawn than an imaginary spook. Maybe she shouldn't leave her sister alone with a strange man. He seemed nice—intelligent, pleasant, even reassuring—but what did she really know about him?

"I'll stay for a while, if you want me to," she agreed.

"I'll help you carry in your luggage," he said.

"Well...all right, but I still don't have a clue about what's going on. What will Gary think about this?"

"He won't like it," Linda admitted sheepishly.

He'll probably have a tizzy-fit, Dawn thought, knowing Gary was impatient with anything the least bit fanciful. Would he blame himself because he left Linda here alone on the outskirts of Ottawa, Wisconsin? The town had had a population of 2,117 when the census sign was painted, and all the stores and businesses occupied two short blocks. Unless she found a job to occupy her time, Linda couldn't be blamed if she started talking to imaginary companions.

Dawn passed through the three doorways that led to the front of the house, feeling the ghost hunter's eyes on her back even though he didn't say anything.

In order to stay, Aaron knew he might have to win the approval of this stunning but skeptical woman. Linda wanted him there, but would she insist on it if her sister objected?

He followed her outside, admiring what he saw in spite of his uneasiness about her opposition. She was light-footed, gliding rather than walking down the steps and across the lawn to a black van parked in the driveway. Dressed for travel in stone-washed jeans and a pale cream tank top, she managed to look sleek and fashionable in a way that had nothing to do with clothing. He found himself wishing he'd met her in a less tense situation.

The sun was warm, but it didn't account for the sheen of perspiration forming on his forehead or the moistness of his palms. She was making him nervous, and he couldn't remember the last time he'd felt that way with a woman. He was a college teacher; delectable young coeds draped themselves across his desk with monotonous regularity. His bitterness and anger at Amy, his ex-wife, had served as a shield for several years now. Was he losing his immunity to beautiful women? He hoped not. His life was full and satisfying without a permanent relationship, and he wasn't ready to risk his battered psyche again so soon.

Dawn entered the side door of the van and bent to lift a duffel out from between the seats. He warned himself not to watch, but part of him was enchanted by the graceful way she doubled over and retrieved the bag. She handed it out to him, then turned to grab a garment bag draped over the seat.

"Vans are handy," he said lamely, feeling awkward in the face of her silence.

"I use it for hauling things from auctions and sales," she answered mechanically.

"I know what you're thinking," he said, feeling like a man about to cross a river on thin ice.

"Nothing you want to hear, I'm afraid." She climbed out of the van, ignoring the hand he held out to help her.

"You think I'm a fraud."

"No. You may believe in what you're doing, but I don't want you to do it here. I do think you may have planted the idea of a ghost in my sister's head. She expected something odd to happen, so she misinterpreted some perfectly inno- cent incident."

"I won't deny that's a possibility."

She looked directly at him for the first time since leaving the house, and he racked his brain for something amusing to say to lessen the tension between them. He wanted to see her mouth relax into a warm grin. But he also sensed that the thin ice was cracking under his feet; he had to talk fast or get an icy drenching.

"My main field is psychology, and I'm most interested in helping the victims of paranormal occurrences. I've uncov- ered a number of cases where so-called hauntings were caused by unhappy psyches in living humans. Maybe that's the situation with your sister. If it is, wouldn't it be better to investigate the house, then guide her into coming to that conclusion on her own? Otherwise, she'll be afraid as long as she lives here."

She frowned as he tried to marshal more arguments for continuing his investigation.

"Sometimes I find fraud—people playing tricks on others, or trying to get publicity. I don't think I will here, but there are other explanations. Her pets...."

"Of course! I've always thought having both a cat and a dog is too much. There's nothing paranormal about noisy pets."

"Or the house itself could be the culprit—settling, wind, loose fixtures."

"But what if none of these possibilities can be proven? I don't think you should put more ideas in Linda's head. Everything about this makes me uncomfortable."

"You're not alone. I'm thirty-five, and I've been interested in the paranormal since high school. But I still run into situations that make me uncomfortable. Feeling like an intruder is one. A lot of cases I can dismiss just by reading or hearing what happened, but this one really has me curious. I'll feel guilty if I walk away from it without putting your sister's mind at ease."

"Just look around the house and tell her it's all her imagination."

"She won't be convinced that easily."

"You're not going to do anything totally bizarre—séances or mediums or—"

"Nothing like that."

"I don't want my sister's house written up somewhere. She doesn't need to be an attraction on a psychic bus tour."

He resented the way she was laying down conditions, but admired her for being concerned about her sister. He intended to investigate with or without her approval, but he didn't like the feeling that she was drawing battle lines.

"You're going to stay whether I want you to or not," she said, as if reading his mind.

"It's Linda's decision." He tried to sound mild mannered and agreeable.

"Yes, it's Linda's decision," she said with faint worry lines creasing her forehead. Swinging the garment bag over her shoulder, she moved toward the house in long, graceful strides.

Linda was in the dining room putting a tray on a square oak antique table that had massive bulbous legs.

"You have a new table," Dawn said, wanting to talk about something besides imaginary specters.

"We found it at an auction—and it was one piece Gary didn't need to refinish. Only trouble is, no chairs. That's my summer mission—find a matching set, or maybe six different chairs from the same period."

"Decorators are doing that now—using a collection of different chairs. Complete dining sets this old are hard to find," Dawn said, glad to talk about a safe, familiar subject.

"Let me carry your things upstairs," Aaron offered, taking her garment bag and standing near a curtained exit in the left corner of the room.

"That would be nice of you, Aaron," Linda said, her breathless enthusiasm making Dawn even more uneasy. "You can put them in the big room. You'll love the bed, Dawn. The headboard is carved walnut up to the ceiling. It's been here since the house was new. No owner has been able to figure out how to get it down the stairs, I guess."

"It sounds beautiful," Dawn said, disturbed by Linda's tone of voice as she watched Aaron disappear to go upstairs.

"It will be comfortable. We bought a new mattress. At first we were going to sleep in the big room ourselves, but we fell in love with the view from the back bedroom. There's a balcony—really the roof of the mudroom—and on nice days we have coffee or a drink there after dinner and watch for deer in the woods. The first week we were here a doe and a fawn—"

"It's really a nice home," Dawn interrupted, impatient to talk about the things that were troubling her. "I'm not sure it's a good idea to have him here."

"He seems nice. I squeezed lemons for fresh lemonade, and it will be warm before I get it poured." She laughed self-consciously. "I made some watercress sandwiches, too. Remember when we used to have tea parties? Mom would mix watercress with cream cheese and make tiny sandwiches with all the crusts cut off. I used to love them. Of course, that was before she started cooking full-time at the hospital."

"We were too old for tea parties by then." Linda loved to talk about their childhood, but Dawn preferred to forget it. When they'd received news of their father's death in California two years ago, that chapter of their life closed for her.

Linda had made a snack that resembled their girlhood treat. Dawn ate one sandwich because she was hungry, remembering that Linda liked to work in the kitchen whenever she was really upset.

"What do you know about that man?" she asked, keeping an eye on the green brocade curtain that concealed the stairway.

"I called a friend of Gary's at the university. He only knows Aaron by reputation, but he assured me he really does teach there."

"I wish you'd tell me everything that happened."

Before Linda could answer, Aaron parted the brocade curtain and stepped into the room, his hair ruffled by the edge of the curtain.

He was close enough for Dawn to see a few threads of silver in his thick, wavy hair. She shivered, wondering how it would feel to bury her fingers in the soft strands. This wasn't her usual reaction to men, not even to tall, dark, and handsome ones.

Fantasies like that were as dangerous as they were silly. She dug her nails into her palms and unconsciously squared her shoulders. Whatever he was up to, she had to get to the bottom of it—for her own peace of mind as well as Linda's well-being.

"I want to know what scared Linda into letting you come here."

"I arranged to come before she had her fright."

Dawn gave Linda a meaningful glance. She didn't want to accuse her of imagining things, but it seemed so obvious: he'd planted the idea in her mind! Surely Linda would realize it herself when she started thinking more rationally.

"I want to record everything you can remember, Linda," he explained in a soft-toned voice that disturbed Dawn for no reason she could pinpoint.

Maybe it was because she mistrusted him. If a man was going to sell snake oil, he should sound oily and conniving. Niceness made his deception less forgivable, if he had some ulterior motive for wanting to encourage Linda's imagination.

"Are you going to do that now?" Dawn eyed a tape recorder in a black leather case with unconcealed suspicion.

"Yes. I want you to ignore the recorder and just tell your story, Linda." He sat down between the two women at the square table and helped himself to a watercress sandwich.

"First let me understand something," Dawn said. "You were planning to come here, but when Linda called . . ."

"I thought it was urgent to come right away."

"Did she tell you I was coming, too?"

"Yes."

"How could you possibly think any member of her family would let you suggest more ideas about hauntings?"

"I'm not psychic. I didn't know whether you'd be skeptical or open-minded. And please, don't call it 'haunting.' I investigate unexplained phenomena. Sometimes they can be classified as paranormal—more often not.''

He sat back and sipped lemonade, challenging Dawn with dark, unwavering eyes that made her wonder if he could hypnotize her against her will.

"Can we begin now?" Linda asked. "I'm beginning to think it's not much of a story, after all."

"We'll see. I would appreciate it if you don't comment during the taping, Dawn."

She wanted to tell him to address her more formally; she was uneasy with the intimate way her name rolled off his tongue. His compassionate tone didn't fool her; the man had an actor's mellow, polished voice, but she wasn't going to let him manipulate her sister into imagining she'd seen a ghost. She didn't for one instant trust him, not in the least! Everyone knew there were no such things as ghosts. What was he doing, encouraging Linda to believe in something so medieval?

"Let's start." He activated the machine and his voice became even more professionally soothing. "June eleventh, Ottawa, Wisconsin, home of Linda and Gary Hall. Tell me, Linda, what took place on the night of June eighth?"

"I went to bed around ten-thirty. Gary is in Japan, so I was home alone."

"Where is your bedroom?"

"On the second floor at the rear of the house. I had the windows open—the three overlooking the backyard and the woods. The middle one has a portable screen that's easy to slip out. There's a balcony, but we have to climb up on the window seat and go through the window to get to it. Awkward but fun." She laughed nervously.

"You fell asleep?" His voice was soothing, almost hypnotic, encouraging Linda with unhurried skill.

"Yes. I was dreaming when I woke up suddenly. I don't remember my dream, but it wasn't a bad one."

"What woke you?" He sounded infinitely patient, but Dawn wanted her sister to get to the point. The suspense was becoming unbearable.

"Noise."

"What kind of noise?"

"I'm not sure what to call it. It was muffled at first, then louder and louder. A sound on a wooden floor. A moving, rhythmic noise. There was something familiar about it, but I can't identify it."

Dawn knew her sister was upset, but she hadn't expected the sheer terror that registered on her face. Linda's eyes were wide with fear, and a wet sheen showed on her stark-white forehead.

"Stop! You're scaring her," Dawn protested, knowing even as she said it that Linda was afraid of something she was remembering.

He rose from his chair and reached over, urgently hushing Dawn by putting his fingers over her lips. She didn't have time to resent his high-handed gesture. Linda was talking, and the way she was relating her story was more shocking than the words.

"It was coming from nowhere—everywhere! I was afraid to go to the door. I was sure someone was in the hall. I got to the windows somehow. I had to raise the middle one a little to release the screen and it stuck, but at last the screen fell out onto the balcony. I crawled out. It's tarred. On warm days it gets soft, but it was hard, grainy. I fell ... That's all I remember."

"Did you hit your head? Pass out?" Dawn was more worried than she'd been since Linda's urgent phone call.

"I don't know." Linda shook her head like a swimmer coming up for air. "I was wet. It was raining—storming, really. I thought about lightning hitting the balcony, and somehow I crawled inside. Shut the window. Then I realized I could scream forever and there's no one to hear me.

Our nearest neighbor is at least half a mile away. There are too many trees between houses."

"Oh, honey..." Dawn hurried over to her sister and hugged her. "You must have had a nightmare, after all."

Aaron was shaking his head, trying to stop Dawn from interrupting the flow of Linda's story.

"The noise, Linda. Did you hear it anymore?" he asked.

"No. The house was quiet. Too quiet. I went downstairs. The next thing I remember is calling Dawn—but how could I explain what'd happened? By then I thought it was a dream, but..."

"But what?" he encouraged.

"I was wet—soaked. I didn't think of taking off my wet nightgown until after I talked on the phone. Then I just left it on the kitchen floor and put on the flannel shirt Gary leaves hanging in the mudroom for when he cuts brush. It protects his arms from getting scratched. After that I went to sleep on the living room couch.... Now I'm embarrassed. I brought you both here to hear about my nightmare."

"So it seems," Dawn said, hugging her sister again to show her sympathy.

"Let's not jump to conclusions. Where were your pets?" Aaron asked.

"That's a good possibility," Dawn said, eager to find a more realistic cause than dreams or hallucinations.

"Simba followed me downstairs. She sleeps on my bed when Gary isn't home, but he makes her stay in the mudroom when he's here. He's a dog lover—my cat is only a nuisance to him. He had Lucky before we were married. A golden retriever. He has his own house and a fenced run outside."

"You must have heard Lucky padding around," Dawn said.

"No, he's too rambunctious to come in the house. Also he sheds too much. But he's a good watchdog. No one can get near the house at night without him howling."

"He didn't bark at me in the driveway. I haven't heard a peep out of him since I came," Dawn said.

"He's at the vet's. I took him early this morning for his shots and a checkup. The boy who cleans the kennels is going to return him before dinner to save me the trip."

Dawn ran a hand through her tangle of tawny curls, twisting a lock around her finger. It was an unconscious habit, and she didn't even realize she was doing it until Linda whispered, "Your hair thing."

Aaron shut off the recorder, trying to concentrate on the puzzle Linda had handed him. It was the kind of case he relished: a frightening experience that could be a fantasy— or something else. It fed his curiosity about the paranormal, and Linda needed his help. He didn't doubt that she was genuinely frightened. This was one he couldn't walk away from. With a summer free from academic duties, he could give it his full attention.

He should have been watching Linda, studying her reactions, asking insightful questions. Instead his eyes kept wandering to Dawn. She was fiddling with a strand of hair, working it around her finger as she tried to deal with her sister's experience in a logical way. She's gorgeous and she doesn't have a clue, he thought.

"There's one other thing," Linda said. "I hate to mention it. You probably already think I'm loony."

"No, not at all," he automatically assured her, watching Dawn's hands as she traced the pattern on the lace tablecloth, betraying her agitation with the nervous gesture. Her fingers were long and slender with neatly rounded nails gleaming with clear polish. Her palms were wide, making her hands look strong, not delicate, and he could imagine them glistening with oil, kneading the tense muscles of his shoulders and back.

"I swear they open by themselves," Linda was saying.

With a stab of guilt, he realized he hadn't been listening—nor had he turned the recorder back on.

"Let me get this straight," he bluffed, hoping she'd repeat herself.

"I swear some of the upstairs doors open themselves," Linda obligingly repeated. "We always keep the storage room closed. Why would we want to look at an unfinished junk room?"

"How many times has it happened?" he asked, trying not to watch Dawn as she stood and paced behind the chair where her sister was still sitting.

"Dozens...maybe more. I didn't count. And the bedroom where you're sleeping.... Maybe I shouldn't tell you. I don't want to scare you away."

"You won't do that." He laughed softly. If anything could scare him into leaving, it was the possibility—however remote—of becoming interested in her beautiful but skeptical sister. He was much too satisfied with his unfettered bachelor status to risk another attachment.

"The room where you're sleeping is the worst. I swear that door opens itself every time I close it."

"Maybe it's just a faulty catch, or the floor may be uneven," he said. "That will be easy to check."

Linda yawned. "I'm really glad you're both here, but I'm so sleepy I can hardly keep my eyes open."

"What you need is a nap," Dawn said.

"Your sister is right," he agreed. "I'm only here to help you. Don't worry about treating me as a guest."

"Very kind of you," Dawn said. But the way she said it made him suppress a grin.

Chapter Two

Linda disappeared through the curtained entrance to the stairway, and the dining room was oppressively quiet. Aaron tilted back on one of the wobbly metal folding chairs the Halls were using until they could find ones to match their table. Dawn expected a leg to snap and send him crashing to the floor.

"Our mother never let us tip chairs." She felt silly as soon as she said it. She wanted to question what he was doing, not the way he sat on a chair.

He laughed, easing the tension between them just a little. "Very sensible advice." He brought the chair down on all four legs and leaned forward, his tanned arms on the lace tablecloth.

"If you're open to advice..." she said hesitantly, "I wish you'd get this scary idea out of Linda's head."

"Don't you believe her?"

"I believe she thinks something strange happened. She has a good imagination."

He picked up the tape recorder. "Do you want to hear it again?"

"No! I mean, it's pointless to dwell on it. Linda had a nightmare. I really think you should leave before you give her more ideas."

He watched her closely. She was struggling to keep her voice calm, but he could see sparks of anger that brought out the green in her eyes.

"Do you think I'll harm Linda?"

His question dared her to be honest about the situation, but the habit of protecting her sister was too strong. She refused to back down. "That's exactly what I think. Maybe not intentionally, but I don't think you should encourage her fantasies. She just moved here from a big city. Country life takes some getting used to."

"She seems to love this house."

"Maybe, but Gary is gone a lot, and Linda hasn't found many new friends yet."

"She's friendly—charming. That shouldn't be a problem."

"Maybe not, but she needs to get involved in the real world, not spooky stuff."

He stood abruptly, knocking over the flimsy chair. "The 'spooky stuff' seems real to Linda. You're not taking her fear seriously enough."

She stood, too, facing him across the tabletop. "I'm worried about my sister, but that doesn't mean I believe in something as preposterous as a ghost."

Anger brought a tinge of pink to her cheeks, making her even more attractive, but he fervently wished she'd stayed home instead of rushing to her sister's rescue. Not only was she going to complicate his investigation, she was too distracting for his peace of mind. No woman should look like a goddess when she was acting like an overprotective mother.

"Your sister is an adult, and she seems sensible to me.
When she wants me to leave, I'll go. Until then, I'm going
to do everything I can to put her mind at ease."

Part of Dawn wanted to believe him, but he was too self-
confident, too sure he knew what was right for other people. She needed to prove him wrong and make him admit
there was nothing abnormal—paranormal—about a bad
dream.

Watch out, a little voice warned her. *You could like this
man—a lot.* His smile was warm and winning, but she didn't
want to succumb to the spell he seemed to be weaving.

She straightened her back and held her head higher, unconsciously striking a pose that reminded him of a statue of
Joan of Arc. When he investigated a house, relatives and
friends often hovered around him, offering advice and telling him their theories. When they weren't too pesky, he enjoyed amateur helpers. Dawn was a special case. He might
enjoy her company immensely—if he let himself—but she
seemed determined to dismiss his efforts without a fair
hearing. He was used to skeptics; he just wasn't used to
feeling so attracted to one of his critics.

He toyed with the idea of leaving, but the opportunities
to investigate genuine phenomena were few and far between. As long as he could proceed without harming Linda,
he wasn't going to give up on this case. Backing away from
a situation like this would prey on his mind for years. He
would always worry that he'd deserted a woman who really
was being tormented by the paranormal.

"I won't let you take advantage of my sister," she
warned, making up her mind to watch every move he made.
If he wasn't what he claimed to be, Linda could be in danger. Did he want to exploit the situation in some way?
Maybe he even intended to fake more so-called phenomena
to build his own reputation as a ghost hunter.

"That's understood. I have nothing to hide."

"How do you go about...?" She groped for a better name for his ghost hunting.

"Investigating? The first step is to explore the house from top to bottom, inside and out."

"Just look around, you mean?"

"Basically, yes. I need to eliminate physical causes for the phenomena—tree branches scraping the house, animal pests... Once I found a raccoon who liked to sleep on a roof."

"I suppose that makes sense."

Gary wasn't home enough to handle the outside work, and Linda might not notice something that needed fixing. She didn't do jobs like cleaning the eaves or running the gas mower. Gary hired them done when he was gone.

"I want to get as much accomplished as possible before dark. If you'd like to tag along, let's get started."

She would probably watch every move he made. He wasn't going to make her even more suspicious by trying to stop her, but he would show her the gritty and tedious side of ghost hunting and hopefully, wear her out. Maybe she wouldn't be watching his every move for the rest of the investigation.

Dawn envied her sister, napping on this warm, humid afternoon. She needed a shower and a few hours of snoozing herself, but she wasn't going to shut even one eye while the ghost hunter was prowling the house.

"Since Linda's sleeping upstairs, let's do this floor and the basement, then go outside." He walked toward the living room without waiting for her approval.

For a guest, he was awfully nervy: opening the window seat, looking behind the couch, climbing on a shaky folding chair to investigate a hanging light fixture. He bent and stretched, proving one thing to Dawn: he had a lithe, athletic body with a tight, round bottom, a lean waist and muscular shoulders and arms.

"What are you looking for?"

"I bet your mother told you not to stand on folding chairs," he said, ignoring her question and coming down with a thump loud enough to trigger another of Linda's nightmares.

"She also said it isn't polite to snoop in other people's homes."

"Your mother didn't have a ghost, did she?"

"Of course not! Neither does Linda. And you said to call it 'paranormal activity.'"

"You listen better than my students."

"I'm older than your students," she said, a half smile playing around the corners of her lips.

He wiped his hands on the sides of his jeans to get rid of dust from the light fixture. He'd liked looking down on her from a chair; in fact, he liked looking at her from every angle. He found himself cataloging her assets instead of concentrating on the problem at hand. Her face wasn't conventionally pretty, but it wasn't one a man was likely to pass without a second look. He loved the way her cheekbones accentuated her eyes, making her look faintly exotic.

He spent more time than she thought necessary in the room beside the living room, even opening drawers in Gary's desk and turning the TV on and off several times.

"I think you're doing all this just to demonstrate how thorough you are." None of this seemed real—not Linda's story, not his interest in the paranormal, and certainly not her self-appointed role as watchdog to a man who made her think of candlelight dinners and dancing under the stars, romantic daydreams she'd long ago filed away under teenage fantasies.

If the house had air-conditioning, it wasn't on. Her hair was sticking damply to the back of her neck, and her jeans felt as warm as ski pants.

"Didn't you see the bit on TV where a cat kept stepping on a remote control, making the television come on mysteriously when no one was in the room?" he asked.

"No. What programs do you watch, children's shows?"

"I'll watch almost anything for a few minutes. I call it cultural sampling."

"I guess that makes you a television Don Juan—never one to settle down." She flushed when she realized she was flirting. Whatever his tastes, she'd never seen anyone who looked less like a TV addict. There was no couch-potato spread on his tautly rounded backside, and his stomach was as flat as a board.

After spending enough time in the family room to repaint it from ceiling to floor, he went into the foyer and tested the hooks on the hall rack, wondering if she'd grow bored with his unnecessarily tedious inspection. He did want to make a thorough search of the house and grounds, but her close scrutiny was making him feel like a suspect in a felony. Or was he only uncomfortable because her top was damply clinging to her bosom, clearly showing the outline of her lace-edged bra, making him feel like a schoolboy stealing furtive glances?

"Gary refinished this hall rack," she said. "He has a passion for redoing old furniture."

"It's a nice Victorian piece, isn't it? I like this slot for umbrellas." They both bent their heads at the same time, quickly backing away when they realized how close they were.

On the porch, the glider seemed to fascinate him. He sat on the center cushion and made it swing back and forth, paying particular attention to the chains attached to the ceiling.

"Hanging from the beams," he said, still energetically swinging. "Here, sit by me. Let's see if it's any noisier with two."

She complied, telling herself it was only to hurry him along. She certainly didn't want to swing with him. His knee brushed hers when they both rose at the same time, and she thought it was unfair that a ghost hunter didn't look more like Frankenstein's monster and less like a swashbuckling hero.

"Almost hypnotic, isn't it?" he asked as they both watched the glider slow down and finally stop.

"Is hypnotism one of your interests, too?"

"Don't worry," he said with a furtive grin. "I'm not a hypnotist. And if I were, I'd need a little cooperation from you to unlock your secrets."

"You wouldn't find any exciting ones, anyway. Is it really necessary to examine every inch of this house?" She was beginning to wonder if he were playing games for her benefit. "Are you doing this to prove something to me?"

"Partly," he admitted. "I've had some experience winning over skeptics."

Cool it, he warned himself, wondering why her opinion seemed so important. He knew it was best to keep things impersonal, but he had the uncomfortable feeling more was at stake than a chance to do a paranormal investigation.

"Now the basement," he said briskly, stopping in the kitchen to arm himself with a flashlight he'd brought in from his Jeep.

Basements weren't her favorite places, and this one rated high on her scale of creepiness. It was divided into little cubicles and hidey-holes, and the unfinished ceiling was a paradise for spiders, her least-favorite creatures on earth.

"The noise couldn't come from here," she said, hoping to hurry him along, but still determined to see that he didn't do anything to the house to make it seem haunted. He was a charmer, but didn't all good con men have winning ways?

"The basement is always the first place I suspect," he said, nonchalantly brushing away a filmy web that caught in his hair. "Plumbing is always suspect—air in the pipes, loose fittings."

He could sense her suspicion and see it in her narrowed eyes. He had to deal with skeptics whenever he got involved in the paranormal, but it would be a real handicap to his investigation if he spent all his time trying to prove things to her. His best hope was that she would grow bored with the tedium of examining the house. Or maybe the army of spiders bivouacking in the rafters would scare her away.

"Look! Copper tubing. That means it's not the original plumbing, doesn't it?" Gary had mentioned new plumbing as one of the selling points of the house. "Maybe there are some noisy loose connections."

"Maybe." He ducked under a low heating duct coming from the furnace and disappeared from sight. "Tap right here for me, will you?"

"Okay." Apprehension was making her thirsty, but no way would she run up for a glass of water and let him plant a noisemaker or something else to make his ghost theories more plausible.

"Tap a little harder. I'm listening for an echo."

"What are you doing back there?"

"Better come back and see for yourself. Watch your head."

She didn't know what was more ludicrous: his inspection or her watchdog activities. Ducking low, she still bumped her shoulder on the duct. Worse, her head butted into his midsection when she came through. He grunted in discomfort, and she muttered an embarrassed apology.

Nothing was behind the furnace but a crudely built shelf against the wall and a tiny amount of floor space barely large enough for them to stand without touching. In the dim light from his flashlight, she made out some empty glass jars and a rusty hose attachment to sprinkle lawns.

"There's nothing back here." They were so close she automatically whispered.

"I agree."

He swung his light around, and the bulb went out.

"What's wrong with your flash?"

"Batteries, maybe." He shook it, but nothing happened. "I seem to be jinxed today. Or maybe it's because I left on such short notice, I didn't have time to check out my equipment."

She couldn't see, but all her other senses went into overdrive. She could smell his spicy cologne, combined with a pleasant male musk. His breathing was soft and even, and she could imagine the breath filling his lungs under the muscular swells of his chest. He clicked his tongue, a teasing sound that made her think of his firm, sensual lips and wonder how they would feel pressed against hers.

He was smiling in the dark, wondering how his little watchdog liked this part of ghost hunting. He hadn't sabotaged his flash, but he couldn't have planned a better way to discourage her. The only trouble was, his imagination was running away with him. The faint, flowery smell of her hair made him want to run his fingers through it. They were so close that the slightest movement would earn him a penalty for bodily contact. Here was his chance to play hero and lead a lady in distress to safety, or he could exaggerate their plight and give her a good scare to get her out of his hair.

His arm brushed hers, and the contact was electrical. He rarely felt in danger in his paranormal investigations, but Dawn had set off his warning system. This woman could easily get under his skin—and not because of her skepticism.

"Let me help you," he said, putting his hand on her shoulder and slowly running it down the length of her arm until he cupped her hand. "The only trick is to not bump your head."

The dark hole behind the furnace didn't seem so scary when he held her hand like that.

"Turn around and stoop down. I'll put my hand on your head so you don't bump it on the duct."

"You really don't need to..."

She liked the way his hand felt resting on her head, his fingers buried in her hair.

"Go forward now. You should be all right."

Duck walking wasn't dignified, and she was glad he couldn't see any better than she could. He did guide her head under the duct without a bump, but she thought he was being overly helpful when he ran his hand down her back all the way to her bottom as she escaped from the cubicle. She nearly protested, then decided to save her ammunition for something really important: his ghost hunting.

He owed her an apology—and he wouldn't blame her if she slapped his hand—but he liked what he'd felt. He did admire a round, firm backside, and she filled her jeans to perfection.

She knew the difference between a helping hand and a pat on the rear, but she bit back her protest. She wanted to catch a fraud, not create a scene. But she was keeping score. Dr. Aaron Mead had better watch his step—and she'd better be very careful not to enjoy it when his warm brown eyes sized her up and his smile made her feel like Cinderella at the ball.

He didn't see anything out of the ordinary in the rest of the basement, but he spent another twenty minutes checking the catches on windows, looking under an old square of linoleum on the cracked cement floor, and testing the sturdiness of cupboards and shelves. She stuck with him, quiet except for an occasional dust-induced sneeze, and he had to give her high marks for perseverance. She wasn't going to let him get away with anything. Her suspicions could become a nuisance, but for now he was actually enjoying their game of cat and mouse.

After having her go up and down the open steps twice to test their sturdiness, he had mercy and called off the basement part of his investigation.

The kitchen was considerably warmer than the basement, but it was good to get out of the musty depths. He smiled at a dark smudge of dirt on her cheek and reached out to flick a bit of debris from her hair.

"Not a spider!" she cried out.

"No, nothing living."

Dawn looked around at the kitchen, not quite ready to meet his gaze that lingered on her while they drank tap water from heavy white mugs. Linda had given a glowing description on the phone of her fully renovated kitchen, and she hadn't exaggerated. With two ovens, a huge refrigerator-freezer, a harvest table large enough for ten, and enough counter space for a restaurant, the only drawback was that it looked much more modern than the rest of the house. After prowling around in the basement, modern seemed very nice.

"You might want to wash your face before I check the mudroom," he suggested.

Needing a minute to think through her situation, she readily agreed, and went into the bathroom off the kitchen. It was the largest one she'd ever seen. Even with an entire wall of cupboards on one side and a huge claw-footed tub, there was room for a set of square dancers to go through their paces in the open space. When she came out, he invited her to watch him check the room's plumbing.

"There is air in the pipes," he said, "but Linda must be used to hearing them."

* * *

Aaron was as thorough in the mudroom as he had been everywhere else, but he didn't try to conceal anything he was doing.

"Can't you skip over anything?" she asked.

"Afraid I'm a born snoop. When I'm not doing this, I haunt flea markets and garage sales looking for things like magic tricks and old photographic equipment. Let's see what's outside."

He found what he wanted in the barn that served as a garage: two lengths of sturdy wooden ladder that clamped together to reach the highest part of the house. Dawn made two trips helping him carry it to the far side of the house.

"Maybe you'd better stay on the ground. You can hold the ladder for me," he suggested.

"You're investigating the roof?"

"I need to check for damaged eaves, dangling antennas, lightning rods, loose shingles, tree branches hitting the house...."

"Then I'm coming up too." She wasn't fond of heights, but the roof seemed like the perfect place to plant some kind of noise-making device.

He climbed with the agility of a high-wire performer, but she wasn't as confident of her own ability to reach the sloping roof.

"Are you sure you want to come up?" he called down, sitting to hold the top of the ladder while she climbed.

She took a deep breath, wondering what kind of chase he was leading her on. How did she know a rung wouldn't break? What if the two parts of the ladder weren't firmly locked together? What if it swayed away from the house while she was climbing?

"One, two, three..." Counting made it easier, but when she reached the second, slightly narrower section of the ladder, her nerve started to fail her.

She raised her eyes enough to see the lower half of his body perched on the edge of the roof, waiting for her.

"You don't have to do this," he said, wondering how he would live with himself if she panicked and fell.

His encouragement to quit was all the incentive she needed to go on. Forcing herself not to look down, she inched her way up until his hand was within reach.

"I didn't think you'd do it." He was sweating bullets and his arms felt shaky. Heights didn't bother him, but her hesitation had given him a real scare. Maybe he should quit leading her on this search before the game got out of hand.

"How am I going to get down?" She was scared and didn't care if he knew it.

"Haven't you climbed this high before?"

"No, we grew up in a one-story duplex. I used to help Mom clean the eaves, but it wasn't so—" She made the mistake of looking down, and her knees turned to water.

"It is high. I'll talk you down and then walk up to the peak to check things."

"No. I'll watch while you do what you came up here to do."

"Well, stay where you are. Don't move and you'll be fine," he said, wishing the spiders in the basement had done the job of discouraging her.

She watched as he moved to the highest elevation, sure-footed as a cat on the steep slope. Whatever else he was, he wasn't clumsy. Quickly satisfied, he came back to her.

"Move your right foot down one rung. Don't worry, I'll hold the top of the ladder firm."

He was shouting to be heard by the time she finally put a foot on solid, grassy ground. She took a deep breath and backed away from the ladder, watching until he was down by her side.

"Dawn, I'm sorry."

"Sorry?" She was embarrassed. It wasn't like her to take risks—or to fail.

"It's hot. You're tired. I shouldn't have let you climb so high."

"You didn't let me. I've climbed ladders before. I just didn't realize how steep this roof is." He knew it was his fault. Annoyed by her attitude, he'd goaded her into going everywhere he went. "I apologize, anyway," he said.

"Is all this poking around a sham?" she asked suspiciously. "Is that why you feel guilty? You're leading me on a wild-goose chase, aren't you?"

"No, not entirely. I always make a thorough house check."

"But?"

"But maybe I've been a little too thorough today. At any rate, this is it for now. I'll check the upstairs later."

"I knew there was no reason to flip all those light switches on and off, on and off, on and off..."

He watched as she retreated into the house. His strategy had worked—or had it? She was out of his hair for the moment, but not out of his mind.

Upstairs she found the room where Aaron had left her bags. Linda was right about the bed. The carved headboard nearly touched the ceiling, dwarfing the mattress part of the bed. Except for a card table and another folding chair—they must have bought a truckload at an auction or bankruptcy sale—there was no other furniture. She knew furnishing a guest room wasn't a high priority for new homeowners, but it was a little creepy to be in such a large, empty bedroom.

As huge as the room was, there were only two small windows, one overlooking the front porch and the other on the side of the house. The linen shades were drawn halfway to the sills and nondescript sheer curtains hung limply beside them. She knew what to give Linda for her birthday in September: custom-made drapes and a matching spread for this room. With pale, oily green walls and bare wooden flooring, it was the coldest room she'd ever seen.

The closet at the far end was a small room in itself with rods hung the length of two sides and storage cabinets at the rear. It was larger than her three closets combined; in fact, her whole apartment would almost fit into this single room. Linda hadn't exaggerated the size of the house, but she hadn't explained why she'd wanted such a large place.

Too weary to care at the moment, Dawn carried her duffel into the hallway, locating a pleasantly modern bathroom next to her room. It was probably a converted closet, but the ivory fiberglass shower stall was the most inviting feature of the house at this moment. She stripped and made a bundle of her soiled clothes, then shampooed under the shower and let the spray pelt her skin until she finally felt clean and as relaxed as possible under the circumstances. Dr. Aaron Mead was maddening, exasperating.... Words failed her, but she wished she could get him out of her head.

She dressed in the bathroom, pulling on white knit shorts and a turquoise scoop-neck top. After trading her tennis shoes for a pair of thongs, she padded back to her room where at least the bed was inviting. She lay down on the faded pink-and-lime quilt that had once covered one of the twin beds in the room she and Linda had shared as children. The threadbare cotton was as soft as down, and in seconds she was sound asleep.

Something woke her—a voice that pulled her out of a deep-sleep cycle. At first she didn't know where she was, and then she thought it was morning.

"It's me," Linda said softly from the open doorway. "Sorry I startled you. Thought you'd want to wake up for dinner."

"Oh, sure. What time is it?"

"Nearly seven. Aaron is doing steaks on the grill. Throwing a bag of charcoal at a man is the best way I know to get out of cooking."

"Aaron." She groaned, wondering if she'd been dreaming about him. His face was etched on her brain, his full, expressive mouth, dark, penetrating eyes, wavy black hair. "I don't trust that man. Are you sure you want him staying here?"

"He's interested in what I experienced, and I'm sure he's not dangerous." Linda sat on the edge of the bed, and Dawn wondered why her sibling was so much more trusting than she was. "You have to admit he's cute."

"That's what you say about your husband."

"It's true. Gary looks just like a little boy when he wakes up in the morning. His hair curls in ringlets when it isn't combed, and he has a sleepy-eyed, pouty look that makes me want to hug and kiss him."

"Thank you for sharing that with me."

"I know how grumpy you are when you nap during the day. I'll be downstairs when you're all the way awake."

The trouble with a sister is that she knows too much about you, Dawn thought. She sincerely hoped Linda wouldn't tell any of her favorite stories—especially the one about Dawn taking her to the neighborhood drugstore and forgetting to bring her home because Mel Hopper gave her a ride on his motor scooter. The pharmacist had given Linda a comic book and a package of candy to keep her from crying while he phoned their mother. Dawn didn't want to be reminded of what she got.

She was uncomfortable with the thought of her sister reminiscing in front of Aaron Mead. The man was like the shell of a popcorn kernel stuck in her gum, like a splinter that hurts but can't be dug out with a needle. She couldn't make him go away—not while Linda was his number one fan—but he made her uneasy.

Linda sometimes accused her of being too much of a feminist for her own good. She wasn't. She enjoyed her male friends and had many casual, friendly relationships with them. It was her good fortune she'd learned early not to put her future in any man's hands. Her father had taught her the first lesson; Brad had given her a post-graduate course when he broke their engagement less than a month before the wedding. Dawn would never forget sending out cancellation notes, returning gifts and selling her wedding dress at a resale shop. She wasn't likely to repeat that mistake—but she wouldn't desert Linda again the way she had in the drugstore.

Linda was finishing a salad in the kitchen when Dawn came downstairs.

"I thought we'd eat here. Cozier than the dining room."

"Fine." Dawn looked around for the ghost hunter with the caution of a mouse watching out for a cat. "Did he tell you about checking out the house?"

"Yes. You really didn't have to go through all that. I remember you never did like heights."

"I was the one who helped Mom clean the eaves."

"But remember when I was chosen to play the bells at church. I wanted to take you up in the tower, but you wouldn't go."

"Those old wooden steps were creaky. I hated to see you going up there."

"The steaks are medium-rare," Aaron said, coming into the kitchen wearing one of Gary's cutesy barbecue aprons and carrying a pewter plate of meat. "I can put them back if they're too red."

He hadn't changed his clothes, but the grubby, wilted look didn't make him unappealing.

"Dawn likes her steak medium-well," Linda volunteered. "Why don't you go out and tell Aaron when yours is done enough?"

"It doesn't matter." She would rather eat raw meat than make a fuss that involved hovering over him while he grilled.

"No problem. I'll just throw one back on." He didn't wait for her supervision.

Aaron did know how to cook a steak—either that or Linda had found a source for the tastiest, tenderest New York strips in the country. He and her sister talked easily, like old friends while they ate. He didn't mention his investigation, but he'd had a chance to do that before Dawn came downstairs.

Linda sounded bright and perky, but her eyes were shadowed and her complexion sallow.

"Do you feel all right?" Dawn asked when they were alone for a moment after supper.

"Funny, I'm still tired, even after that long nap. I guess missing a night's sleep doesn't agree with me."

When Aaron rejoined them, Linda decided to blow up the air mattress they used for camping and sleep in the downstairs room off the dining room.

"It will be cooler down here. Either of you is welcome to use the couch if it's too warm upstairs. We hope to get air-conditioning next summer, but it's not supposed to be so hot here."

She didn't give fear as an excuse for sleeping downstairs.

The long June day was just ending when Linda said goodnight and closed the door on her two guests. Dawn wandered out to the front porch, hoping for a cool breeze and a chance to collect her thoughts alone.

The sluggish air failed to cool her, and Aaron followed in a few minutes, sitting down beside her on the glider.

"I want to warn you . . ." he began.

"No, please, no ghost stories. I'm not going to let you spook me like you have my sister."

"I'm not trying to." He didn't try to hide his irritation now that Linda was out of hearing. "You don't have to talk to me. God forbid, you should laugh at my jokes or help me put your sister at ease during dinner."

"Is that what you were trying to do? It's a little late. She's afraid to sleep in her own bedroom."

"It is cooler downstairs."

"Maybe your ghost wanders all over the house. Maybe he'll come downstairs and . . ."

"Why are you assuming the ghost—your word choice, not mine—is male?"

"I'm not assuming anything. I don't believe such a thing exists."

"Listen, Dawn . . ." He reached out without thinking and put his hand on her arm, quickly withdrawing it before she could protest. Her flesh was warm, almost hot, and he bunched his fist in an unsuccessful effort to forget the silky smoothness of her skin.

"Don't . . ." But he wasn't doing anything, so starting to protest made her feel a little ridiculous.

"All I want to say is . . ." He took a deep breath, inhaling a fresh flowery scent so enticing he wanted to bury his face in her hair to find the source. "Watch out for the electrical cords in the upper hallway. I've installed some equipment to use later tonight. I don't want you tripping and falling. I'll leave the light on."

"You don't need to warn me. I'll be right there watching whatever you do."

They rocked in silence for a long time, but she was too keenly aware of his presence to be comfortable.

The sky had darkened to a deep midnight blue, and he was angry at himself for the flicker of attraction he felt for Dawn. Skeptic or not, she would make his night-long vigil pass much more quickly, but he didn't want this opportunity complicated by his own libido. This was an ideal situation: both past owners and the present resident had experienced something unusual, and as far as he knew, he was the first paranormal researcher to be on site for observation.

"It's time to go to work," he said gruffly.

Upstairs she peeked into the master bedroom. The light from the hallway showed Simba curled up at the end of the bed, a sleek gray-and-white ball of fur too indolent to lift her head and look at Dawn.

"Your mistress is downstairs," she said to the disinterested feline. "A watch cat you're not!"

She sat cross-legged in the doorway of her own bedroom, keeping out of Aaron's way and watching him set up and test his video camera and several other pieces of equipment. Her interest in technology was almost nil, but she was anything but bored. Contrary to her intent—and against her better judgment—she enjoyed watching him work. He didn't putter; everything he did seemed to have a purpose. He wasn't a muscle man with pumped-up shoulders and Popeye arms, but he was magnificently proportioned, not at all the stereotype of a college professor—or a ghost hunter.

If he were mine, I'd curl the hair on the back of his neck around my fingers, she mused in a half-conscious state, straightening abruptly when she realized she was falling into a dreamlike state. Not only that, her seat was numb from sitting on the hard floor.

There was nothing to do but wait, the hardest part of any investigation, Aaron shared with her.

"Is this thing supposed to happen at midnight?" she asked.

"There's no way to know. We could wait here until Christmas and not hear what Linda heard."

"Especially if she imagined it!" She'd been quiet while he'd worked, but she was as skeptical as ever, determined to intervene if he tried to hoodwink her sister in any way. If he intended to get attention for himself by publicizing the house or portraying her sister as a hysterical woman haunted by ghosts, he would have to contend with her first.

"What next?" she asked in a conciliatory tone, realizing she could monitor his activities better if she could keep her doubts to herself.

"I'm taking a thermos of coffee and setting up watch in the storage room."

"Why there?"

"It shares a wall with your sister's room, and the door looks out on the stairwell."

"Why is that important?"

"Let's just say I'm following a hunch. How do you decide whether to stock up on amber necklaces or mechanical robots in your business?"

"I talk to collectors, watch auction results, read the trade papers, and check our own sales. Then I play my hunch and buy what I like," she admitted, laughing at herself.

"If you want me, I'll be in the storage room."

"Oh, no. If anything strange happens, I want to be wide awake in the storage room with you."

"You want to be sure I don't have anything to do with it."

That was true, but she was unexpectedly agitated. She could feel her heartbeat; her pulse was racing as though she were jogging. What she felt was anticipation, not fear, and it had more to do with his very solid, very real existence than anything she expected to see or hear. The hall light was dim, but she could see the tension in his jawline under his silky black beard. She felt on the verge of something extraordinary, a feeling she didn't want to examine too closely. Her very ordinary existence was being challenged, and the only way to see it through was with both eyes wide open.

"Lead the way," she said, recognizing the peculiar feeling low in her stomach for what it was: excitement.

There was one naked bulb lighting the unfinished room Aaron had chosen for his nightwatch.

"I've seen refrigerators with brighter bulbs," she said, determined to keep a lid on her attraction to him.

"Find a spot to sit, then I'll turn it off."

She looked around, not seeing any possibility of comfort. Some of the clutter looked too old and dusty to belong to Linda and Gary. There were several wooden barrels, broken odds and ends of furniture, including a mission-style rocker, and several trunks back in the corner. A number of corrugated boxes, some obviously empty, blocked her view of other potential treasures—or, more likely, trash. They were probably left from her sister's move; their mother had been a box saver, too.

"Linda gave me an old blanket so we won't get quite so dirty. Let me spread it before you sit." He took it from the back of the derelict rocker and stirred up a small dust storm shaking it out.

She spotted a barrel she could use as a backrest and gave him directions between sneezes, watching him spread a threadbare pink-and-purple wool blanket that was vaguely familiar.

"That will work," he said. "We can see through the door."

"Is that all you brought in here, a blanket and a thermos?"

"That's all. Do you want to look around yourself? Check for hidden microphones or..."

"No. What do ghost hunters do while they're waiting?" She sank down to the floor and watched while he flipped off the wall switch and joined her.

"They keep quiet. I can't be everywhere, but my equipment will monitor areas I can't see."

A pale rectangle of light from the hallway showed on the rough flooring by the door, but they were sitting in dark shadows. He offered her some coffee, but she wasn't worried about falling asleep, not while he was so close she could sense the slightest move he made.

"We should have brought pillows," she said, wiggling to get comfortable. Her watch didn't have a luminous dial, but his did. "What time is it?"

She lightly touched his wrist, making his skin tingle.

"Ten-thirty."

"It seems later."

It had been a long day, one so packed with new sensations that she hadn't had time to absorb them. Maybe she'd wake up in the morning and find that Aaron had only been a figment of her imagination, a man she'd dreamed up because the real men in her life had so often disappointed her.

"Hush." He put his finger across her lips in a gesture to silence her, lingering a second longer than necessary as though she might nibble it.

She covered her mouth with her hand, trying to erase the feeling of his touch.

One grimy window showed the dark sky. If the moon was out, it wasn't shining on their watching place. From outside she heard a faint bark. Lucky was out there barking at a raccoon, and this ordinary sound highlighted the oddness of crouching in a dark, dusty room beside a man who believed in ghosts and tried to prove their existence with modern technology. She was less sure than ever that she had any business being there.

The house was alive; it creaked and groaned, but Aaron didn't react to the soft noises of an old structure cooling off or settling down or doing whatever old houses did to make creepy little sounds. She tried counting to reassure herself that time really was passing and she wouldn't be there forever: twenty-one and twenty-two and twenty-three. How high would she have to count before it was sunrise? Her throat was getting dry because she was moving her lips.

Counting wasn't helping; in fact, it seemed to make the time pass more slowly. She tried entertaining herself by imagining all sorts of antique treasures stored in the trunks and barrels that had come with the house. Linda must not have explored them yet. She would have mentioned anything worthwhile to her pack rat sister. She didn't share Dawn's mania for hunting down relics of the past, but she did have a keen appreciation of antiques. Had she explored this room, or was she frightened of it? Had she avoided it even before her big scare?

Dawn tried to see it through her sister's eyes. The bare studs were the skeletal ribs of the house, and the unfinished ceiling showed the slant of the roof above them, the kind of high, murky place beloved of bats, spiders, and horror writers.

She crossed her arms over her chest and pulled up her knees, then quickly straightened out. Curling up in a fetal position didn't exactly fit the image of a hardheaded skeptic!

He noticed, and she could feel his eyes on her in the murky room. She had a feeling he didn't miss much, least of all, signs of nervousness.

He handed her the top of the thermos filled with coffee, his fingers brushing hers.

"Sorry I forgot to bring an extra cup," he said, imagining how it would feel to have her lips on his instead of on the hard edge of the cup.

"It doesn't matter—thanks."

She sipped slowly, trying to make the cupful last as long as possible. When she returned the empty top to him, she knocked against his hand, then tried to convince herself she hadn't done it on purpose. They were so close, her knee bumped against his when she changed position.

Minutes passed like hours. He felt as if he'd been in the dark, dusty room for days, poised for something to happen, but this wasn't like any other watch he'd undertaken. Every time she shifted her weight, she stimulated his imagination. He wanted to lift her off the hard floor and cuddle her on his lap—not a practical idea but one that made him feel like doing some squirming of his own.

It was too still now; even Lucky must be asleep. The house seemed to be waiting, but for what? She shivered even though the dust-laden air was hot. The stifling atmosphere made her giddy—not sleepy, but totally focused on the man beside her. She heard him take a deep breath and had a sudden urge to hear his voice.

"What time is it now?" She reached out, touching his arm so she could see the faint green numerals on his watch, then forgot to look. His fingers curled around hers, leaving out the little one then capturing it so her whole hand was covered by his. She didn't think of pulling it away.

"You don't have to stay," he murmured. "It's nearly four a.m., and this isn't anyone's idea of a fun date."

"I didn't know it was a date. Once a boyfriend took me frog hunting at night."

"There's an idea." He laughed softly.

"I was eleven."

"Too young for boyfriends." He touched her cheek with the back of his fingers.

"Do you think so? When did you have your first crush?" His fingers wandered to the hollow behind her ear, lifting aside her hair then stroking her neck with such feathery lightness she felt oddly cherished.

"Boys don't have crushes," he said.

"I don't believe that."

"Okay, I was in the third grade. Debbie—I forget her last name—started a squirt-gun fight at recess. Or maybe I started it."

"Who won?"

"Neither of us. The teacher on playground duty confiscated our guns. There was no future for us anyway. She was an older woman."

"A fourth grader?"

"Worse—fifth."

"Did you believe in ghosts even then?"

"I believed in things I couldn't see. Everyone does." He wrapped a tendril of her hair around his finger, tugging just hard enough to make her move her face closer to his.

"I don't." It was time for a reality check. If he kept talking in such soothing tones, she'd begin to believe that fairies were parading around the room.

"Of course, you do. Have you ever seen love or compassion or loyalty?"

"You're twisting things around. Emotions aren't the same as things that go bump in the night."

"According to some theories, psychic manifestations are remnants of very strong emotions. Wherever there's an alleged ghost, you'll find a traumatic incident that happened sometime in the past."

"What happened here?"

"I don't know yet, but I intend to find out."

He slid his fingers through her hair, subtly shifting his body so his lips were close to her cheek.

"It's nearly dawn," she said, surprised that she wasn't at all eager to end the vigil. "Do you think something will still happen?"

"No. I think we can call it a night."

He didn't make a move to leave, and she was mesmerized by the soft play of his fingers on the back of her neck.

He was breaking his own fundamental rule of paranormal investigating: don't get emotionally involved, not with the victim and especially not with a skeptical relative whose main interest in the case was to undermine his efforts. But when he'd imposed this restraint on himself, he hadn't met Dawn.

He leaned toward her, gently brushing his lips against hers. A tiny little "Oh" escaped from her mouth, and then he slowly kissed her, savoring the sweet softness of her lips.

"Thank you for watching with me," he whispered.

"But nothing happened."

"Didn't it?" He stood and offered her his hand, pulling her against him as she rose to her feet. "I think we both need some sleep now."

He sent her away with a caress on her shoulder, knowing she had to leave while he was still clearheaded enough to let her go.

Dawn raced down the hall, forgetting about the electrical cords but missing them through blind good fortune.

Closing the door of her bedroom, she threw herself on the bed and bunched the old quilt against her mouth and cheek, too stunned to know how she felt about Dr. Aaron Mead's spine-tingling kiss.

Chapter Three

Why was the ceiling green?

Dawn curled her toes under the sheet and let her eyes focus on the plaster surface above the bed. Ceilings were supposed to be white, not watery lime.

She turned on her side and glanced at her watch, surprised she'd worn it to bed. Stranger still, she was wearing shorts and a top, not her usual short nightie. She closed her eyes, trying to banish the feeling that she wasn't in a real place.

She awoke the second time with a start, sitting upright before she was fully conscious and pulling the wrinkled edge of the sheet up to her chin. Her heart raced as she remembered the night before.

The soft chirping of a bird outside the window roused her to full wakefulness, and memories of the vigil in the storage room flooded her mind. She pulled the covers over her head in embarrassment, but her lips tingled as she remembered Dr. Aaron Mead's intoxicating kiss. She could almost feel the tickle of his beard and the sensual pull of his lips moving against hers. She tried to remember where his hands had been but instead pictured herself running down the hallway like a startled adolescent. She didn't know which memory made her cringe more: being kissed by a ghost hunter she didn't trust or bolting away like a frightened rabbit.

"Oh..." She moaned aloud, dreading the prospect of facing him again.

Remember, he's the intruder here, not you, she reminded herself, swinging her legs over the side of the bed and standing to stretch. The charade was over. She had to convince Linda he was playing mind games with her. The man was a menace.

She ignored the little voice inside her head that asked if Aaron was dangerous to Linda's mental health or her own peace of mind.

He'd slept in worse rooms, but the morning sun was making the front bedroom too warm for comfort. He hadn't begun to have enough sleep, but as soon as he thought of Dawn, there was no chance of dozing off again. Aaron stood by the open window for several minutes, breathing deeply to let the fresh country air chase away his lethargy. The breeze cooled his hot flesh but not his overheated imagination. He felt like rushing to the shower, but he preferred not to cross paths with Ms. Girard.

While he did a few quick stretches to warm up for his morning push-ups, he tried to tell himself he'd only kissed her out of boredom after a long vigil. Unfortunately, he wasn't good at fooling himself.

He heard the creak before he realized what was happening. The door, set in a wide oak frame between two papered yellow walls, was slowly opening. Linda hadn't imagined this phenomenon!

He wasted precious moments pulling on his discarded jeans, deciding he'd have to give up his habit of sleeping nude as long as he was quartered in a room with a door that opened itself.

The paneled oak door had opened inward far enough to allow him to step into the hall without touching it. He was disappointed when it stopped moving, but at least he had a puzzle to solve—something to keep his mind off Linda's sister.

Getting down on hands and knees on the thin gray carpeting in the hallway, he tried to judge the level of the bare oak flooring in the doorway.

Dawn sat in bed trying to decide what to say to Linda. There was no way to get rid of the psychologist unless her sister agreed, but she had to do it without stirring up Linda's passion for matchmaking. If she even suspected what had happened in the storeroom...

Dawn shuddered, remembering Linda's merciless insistence that she go on a blind date with one of Gary's friends a few years ago. Her sister was like a dog with a bone when she got a whiff of romance.

"My love life isn't the issue," she said aloud, resolutely grabbing her robe and heading toward the shower.

Like a pedestrian wary of traffic on a busy street, she looked both ways before stepping into the hallway—and froze.

"Morning exercises?" she asked, trying to pretend there was nothing unusual about a half-dressed man on hands and knees in her sister's hallway.

"The door moved," he said, scurrying to his feet with a guilty start, as though she'd just caught him filching the family silver.

"Oh, sure."

"It opened by itself," he explained lamely. He felt like a fool, and somehow it had to be her fault.

"Did anything odd happen?"

"Depends on what you mean." He gave in to an impulse to tease her, even though he'd been trying hard not to think of her soft, sensual lips parting under his.

"Anything paranormal," she said too emphatically.

He shrugged, wondering if she'd slept in her clothes—or in nothing.

"I went to bed after you left. It wasn't likely anything would happen after daybreak."

"Nothing happened all night, so there's really no reason for you to stay, is there?"

He looked rumpled and sleepy-eyed, the way Linda had described her husband's morning state. Dawn liked the way Aaron's hair fell over his forehead in natural waves, but the curly, fine whorls on his chest really made her feel shivery. His torso was terrific, muscular in all the right places, but she was trying to pretend she didn't notice his half-naked condition. Seeing this sexy man shirtless was too un-nerving, and she tried to keep her eyes focused on the gray-striped wallpaper in the hallway.

"Is there some special reason you want me to go?" Last night he'd acted on impulse and kissed her; now he was be-ing rash—maybe even foolish—in wanting to know more about her, but Dawn had done the one thing he couldn't ig-nore: sparked his curiosity.

"I don't want you taking advantage of Linda just to en-hance your reputation as a ghost hunter."

"That's blunt enough." Instead of angering him, she was fueling his interest. "But what if there is something to fear in this house?"

"I don't believe that," she denied heatedly, wondering if she were the one in real trouble—in danger of losing her head over dark eyes and high, sensual cheekbones. She didn't want to be hurt again; she couldn't pick up the pieces again.

"Give me a little time," he said, backing into his room. "Believe it or not, this door opened itself, and I want to know why."

Aaron's door was closed when she came out of the shower, and it was still shut when she left her room to go downstairs. Her crisp pink cotton shorts seemed to wilt instantly in the humid air trapped in the stairwell, and her matching tank top was already sticking to her midsection.

"Good morning. I didn't expect it to be so hot in Wisconsin," she said, finding Linda in the kitchen standing in front of an open oven and testing a breakfast casserole with a fork.

"It's my first summer here," she reminded Dawn, "but I guess we have to expect a few hot spells. I'm beginning to wish we'd put in air-conditioning this year."

"You look really beat," Dawn said. "Didn't you sleep well?"

"Yes, I did. It helped a lot to know the two of you were upstairs. I slept fine."

Dawn raised one eyebrow to register her disbelief, but Linda turned her attention to buttering toast that had just popped up.

"There's really no reason to have Aaron here," Dawn said.

"It can't hurt—just to satisfy my curiosity."

"There's probably some perfectly logical explanation for everything that happened. When Gary gets here . . ."

"I have something important to tell you." Linda sat down at the large harvest table set with green checkered place mats and yellow-flowered stoneware plates.

"You sound serious. What's wrong?"

"Nothing. I'm just a little shaky this morning."

"There's something you're not telling me."

"Yes, but it's good news. I'm going to have a baby!"

"A baby!" Dawn squealed and hugged her sister, so excited she couldn't contain her exuberance. "When is it due? When did you find out? Do you have a good doctor? How are you going to decorate the nursery? Do you want a boy or a girl? I'm going to be an aunt!"

"You're going too fast. I only confirmed it yesterday. I took Lucky to the vet, and then I went to the doctor."

"I'm so happy for you. What did Gary say?"

"I haven't told him yet... it will make it much harder for him to be away so much. For now, let's just keep it between the two of us. I feel a little guilty not telling him first. We both want a baby so much."

"Okay, but I'll probably spill it all to Jane when I get back. I'll have to tell someone or burst!"

"You will stay your whole vacation, won't you?"

"Of course. There's no place I'd rather be. When the ghost hunter leaves, we'll have a million things to talk about."

"Good morning." Aaron stepped into the kitchen, immediately aware that he'd interrupted something. "I hope you didn't wait breakfast for me."

The three of them ate without much conversation beyond discussing the weather and food, then lingered over coffee at the kitchen table. Aaron waited for Linda to question him, not sure how much Dawn had told her about the previous evening.

"I guess if the two of you had experienced anything unusual last night, you would tell me," Linda said, refilling their cups with the air of someone who was ready to tackle important matters.

"We didn't experience anything... paranormal," Aaron said with a quick glance at Dawn.

"Absolutely nothing," she agreed, still excited enough about the baby to dance around the kitchen and hug everyone in sight—no, terrible idea. The news wasn't hers to share, and Aaron was off-limits for hugging. If she had any sense at all, she'd put as much distance as possible between herself and Dr. Mead.

Aaron and Linda talked in circles for ten minutes, then twenty, but Dawn dropped out of the conversation, preferring cleanup duty to participation in their bizarre discussion about things that go bump in the night. She couldn't go home and leave Linda alone with him, especially not now when Linda was pregnant and lonely for Gary, but she refused to buy into their fantasy.

A crumpled paper napkin on one of the plates suddenly fluttered, danced across the counter, and flew to the floor. Dawn was startled, but, thankfully, the other two were too busy talking to notice her reaction. She looked around the kitchen and saw the cause: an open window over the sink. All their talk of paranormal happenings must be getting to her—or else she was jumpy from lack of sleep. One little kiss couldn't be responsible for making her so edgy.

Whatever Linda thought she'd experienced, there was a logical explanation for it, just as there had been for the mysterious flying napkin.

She shook her head and left the room, remembering the new paperback book nestled between her shorts and nightie in her duffel.

The glider on the front porch was designed for leisurely summer reading, and Dawn made herself comfortable, balancing the book on her knee. Most of her reading time was spent on antique trade publications and price guides, and it was sheer joy to hide away with her favorite historical author. She liked her fantasies clothed in shimmering satin gowns and velvet doublets, not rotting shrouds or blood-soaked rags.

The book was promising: a hero with rippling muscles and a heroine with an agonizing secret. She opened it to page one and read the first paragraph—four times.

She couldn't pretend she was on vacation, and she couldn't relax not knowing what Aaron was up to. Reluctantly she put aside her book. At least Linda's wonderful news about the baby made the trip worthwhile. She didn't regret not going to Virginia to visit and go antiquing.

She found Aaron in the storage room looking hot and rumpled in wrinkled khaki shorts and a T-shirt with a university logo. She had an urge to moisten her finger and rub away a smudge of dirt on his forehead, but she mentally slapped her hand. There wasn't going to be a repetition of their kiss, and the mushy feeling she got looking at him was probably only the heat.

"Are you keeping busy?" she asked.

"This room has happy memories for me," he said with a grin, dropping a pile of papers on the seat of the old rocker.

She blushed but didn't have an answer to that.

"I'll apologize if you like," he said, stepping closer. "You're a beautiful woman, Dawn, but I was out of line. I do have professional ethics."

"As a psychologist?"

"Yes. Although I spend more time teaching than in private practice."

"What I meant was, are you here as a psychologist? Do you think of Linda as your patient?"

"Not exactly. I'm trying to answer questions that bother me. There's no doubt in my mind that unexplained phenomena actually happen. Someday I think we'll have some answers. If I can contribute anything toward that end, then my investigations are worthwhile. But even if this turns out to be a dead end, I'll be satisfied if I can put Linda's mind at ease."

"You make it sound logical—helpful, even. But nothing—paranormal—happened last night. What are you going to do now?"

"Before I get into it, let's talk." He scooped the stack of papers from the rocker and piled them on the floor, making room for her to sit.

She sat, being careful not to cause an avalanche with the precarious piles surrounding the chair. She had a peculiar feeling, but it wasn't one she could analyze.

"Let me give you a little background on the history of ghosts," he said.

"Is this going to be a lecture, Professor?" she teased, wishing she didn't enjoy the mellow tone of his voice quite so much.

"Probably," he agreed, grinning. "But hear me out, please.... Even prehistoric humans in Stone Age cultures seem to have believed in ghosts," he began slowly, putting his foot on a barrel and leaning close. "They buried all kinds of useful things for their dead to take along—food, clothing, weapons, sometimes even wives or servitors."

"That's gruesome."

"True, but beside the point. As soon as Homo sapiens started believing in an afterlife, they probably began wondering if their deceased could come back. Maybe, when they got high on whatever the medicine man was pushing in their tribe, they thought they saw the spirits of the dead."

"So prehistoric ghosts were drug-induced illusions?"

"I'm only trying to convince you I didn't invent them."

"Aren't you perpetuating a myth by being a ghost hunter?"

"What I do is investigate. Maybe I'm a little obsessed, but it's live people that fascinate me. Their minds do strange and sometimes wonderful things. I want to know why people have been seeing paranormal phenomena for thousands of years."

"No one has ever proven there's such a thing."

"But almost no one denies there are occurrences that frighten people, things outside the natural order. When I investigate paranormal happenings, I use skills I learned in ten years of university work. Most of the time I can put people's minds at ease."

"I'm not comfortable with this."

"I know."

Her hair was swept up into a ponytail, girlish but cute. He realized she was one of those rare women who don't need hair dangling around their face to enhance their beauty.

"I wish Linda wasn't involved in this."

Dawn still didn't trust him; he could see it in her eyes and the set of her mouth. What would he have to do to convince her he wasn't a fraud with an agenda of his own?

"What are you doing with all these papers?" she asked.

"Hoping to learn more about the earlier residents of the house. Most of these date back to the first family to live here."

"They smell musty." She picked up a bundle of letters tied with a faded lavender ribbon. "I'm surprised Gary and Linda didn't clean this room out."

"They probably intended to later. Haven't they done quite a bit of work on the rest of the house?"

"They've totally redone parts of it. Why would any of this help you?" She opened an old scrapbook and discovered pages of keepsakes: photos, dance programs, newspaper clippings, and locks of dark hair in a dry, crackly glassine envelope.

"The people who owned this house before your sister and brother-in-law did some research of their own. Those notebooks with the speckled black-and-white covers are theirs—old newspaper clippings, handwritten notes and parts of letters. They've done some of my work for me."

"I wonder why they left the notebooks behind."

"I can only guess. Maybe they were so relieved to be getting out of the house, they didn't want to take along any reminders."

"What have you found so far?" She was more interested than she wanted to be.

"I'm only beginning. I'm going to carry it all downstairs and spread it out on the dining room table."

"Let me help you."

For a moment he was too surprised to answer.

"I'm used to handling ephemera," she said. "Postcards, old trade cards, odds and ends like nineteenth-century diaries and autograph books. All kinds of stuff."

What she told him was true, but she couldn't help but hope her participation would speed up his investigation. She just wasn't comfortable with the idea of paranormal occurrences.

"I think you'll be a big help."

Dawn helped him haul the piles downstairs and sort them into manageable stacks on newspapers spread on the table. Much to her surprise, she found herself enjoying the intimacy of working with him. He gave serious consideration to everything she pointed out as she read through a huge pile of odds and ends, everything from old canceled checks to an elementary school report card that had been torn in two and repaired with cellophane tape that fell off when she touched it.

"Look at this bill of sale," she said, handing him a paper so creased it was in danger of falling apart. "The Jensens must have owned half of the county at one time. Are they the original owners of the house?"

"Yes. Louisa Jensen married Carl Hoover, and this house was a wedding present from the bride's father. I haven't learned much about Carl, but he seems to have worked for Mr. Jensen."

"Louisa married her father's hired help? Do you suppose they were happy?"

"I don't know, but in many cases, there are dysfunctional families associated with paranormal manifestations."

"Ghosts tend to come from unhappy families?"

"I couldn't have said it better myself," he said grinning.

She worked hard, laboriously reading every document and scrap of paper, sorting out exactly the kind of data he wanted. After checking the first few things she handed him, he felt completely confident in her judgment.

"How long do you think this will take?" She wasn't complaining. Hot and grubby as she felt, she also felt a deep sense of satisfaction working with the mementos of a past time—and working with Aaron.

He wanted the job to last for days, weeks, months. She was immensely helpful, but she was also a distraction. When a strand of hair came out of the band holding her ponytail, he wanted to tuck it back and press his lips to the creamy spot of skin at her nape. She was dressed in casual shorts and top, but they didn't disguise her soft, feminine curves. She sat on the floor after a while, making piles on plastic garbage bags spread out to protect the carpet. Her feet were tucked under her bottom, and her smooth thighs were displayed without any obvious intent to beguile. He spent more time looking at her than at the faded ink on the letter he was trying to read.

Leave it to him to be attracted to a woman who only wanted to get rid of him!

"What are you two doing?"

Linda stepped into the dining room, startling Dawn so much she nearly bumped heads with Aaron. They were both on the floor, boxing up papers they no longer needed in one of the cartons left from the Halls' move.

"Sorting papers from the storage room," Dawn said self-consciously, afraid of what Linda the Matchmaker would think of their cozy scene.

"What did you find out?" Linda's hair was a mass of blond curls, and she was wearing crisp white shorts and a red polka-dot tank top that made her look cool and relaxed.

"Quite a bit," Aaron said, pulling Dawn to her feet, doing it with so little effort he made her feel like a featherweight.

"Then why not tell me during lunch? It's all ready."

"I need to wash off some grime," Aaron said, leaving the room.

Linda rummaged through some papers still on the table, picking up a bundle of household receipts, then quickly dropping them and rubbing her fingers together as though she were flicking away dust.

"How can you sort through all this?" she asked. "I wanted Gary to haul most of the stuff in the storage room to the dump, but I knew you would worry that we might have thrown away something valuable."

"Dawn understands the historical value of old paper," Aaron said, returning to the room.

"She always was the brainy one in the family," Linda said with pride.

Dawn looked at her own hands, then excused herself to wash them in the bathroom off the kitchen. She didn't feel in the least bit smart. Was it bright to let herself work so closely with Aaron? Helping him would get him out of the house sooner, and that was her goal; she just wished she didn't enjoy his company so much.

Her hands were so grimy from old newsprint and dirt, she had to wash them twice before they felt clean.

Admit it, you're not lucky with men, she told herself, avoiding her image in the mirror over the sink. She knew how she looked: hot and disheveled, with a face that wouldn't stop traffic on her best days. Aaron might be mildly attracted, but pretty soon he'd be on his way. If she expected nothing from him, she wouldn't be disappointed.

And there was still that ghost thing.

Linda was the only good cook in their family. Their mother had had a genius for making everything taste like cafeteria food, and Dawn's idea of food preparation was to open a can of tuna and mix it with mayonnaise. One of the nice things about visiting Linda was her cooking. She complimented the meal, and Aaron praised the three-bean salad extravagantly, but Linda was more interested in their findings.

"I'm dying to know what you learned," she said, putting a plate of homemade chocolate cookies on the table.

"We know a little about the family who originally lived here but not enough to know what might have caused a paranormal occurrence."

Dawn tried to catch his eye to warn him off. Linda was upset enough without wondering if something bad had happened in the house in the past. But it was too late to cut him off. Anything she could say now would only increase Linda's curiosity.

Aaron knew Dawn was frowning at him, but he pretended not to notice. She didn't want him to say anything to further pique her sister's curiosity, but it was Linda's house and Linda's problem. He had an obligation to tell her what he knew. If the manifestations were wholly psychological, he might be able to put Linda's mind at ease and eliminate her fear. If there were more complicated reasons for what she had heard, he could at least make the incidents seem harmless, which he sincerely believed they were. All old houses had strange noises: creaks, moans, and shudders. None were consequential unless they caused distress for the people living there.

"First, doors that open themselves," he said. "I saw it happen myself. The floors upstairs aren't level, whether from warping or careless construction, I don't know. The doorjambs are slightly warped, too. My guess is the house may have sat empty for a winter or two with little or no heat. That can take a heavy toll on any building. Anyway, a good carpenter can help you with the doors. Or you can use doorstops."

"That's good news. Maybe I'll try to find a doorstop. I saw a cast-iron Boston Terrier at an auction," Linda said. "Gary might get a kick out of one like that. What about the ghost?"

Aaron looked uncomfortable now.

"I try not to use that word when I'm investigating an incident that could be paranormal," he reminded her.

"Paranormal is a scary word to me," Linda said. "It reminds me of kids around a campfire telling ghost stories."

Linda wasn't going to give up on that word, Dawn realized, feeling her first touch of good humor since Aaron had started his tortuous explanation.

"About the family," she said, not quite able to stay completely out of it because she was still worried about Linda.

"The first family to live here suffered through some bad times. Carl Hoover married the daughter of his wealthy employer, and this house was their wedding gift," Aaron began.

"In stories the heiress usually gets disinherited when she marries a poor man," Linda said.

"I don't know how Carl got along with his father-in-law, but he seems to have prospered. The tragedies began when they had children. They lost the first three when they were very young, apparently from childhood diseases."

"You didn't tell me about the children dying," Dawn said, wanting to distance herself from such an unhappy narrative.

"It was in Louisa's diary. I thought reading it would be depressing work for you."

He was right, but she was vaguely hurt. They hadn't really been sharing in the work. He was probably used to graduate students slaving for hours on his projects just for the honor of working with him. She'd only imagined that they'd established a good working relationship.

"The Hoovers didn't give up. Their fourth and last child survived the dangerous early years. Carl Junior."

Linda had an anxious frown, and Dawn quickly tried to reassure her. "In those days they couldn't do much about diseases. It's much easier to raise healthy children today."

"Then there was a happy ending of sorts," Linda said.

"That's as far as I've gotten. I'm hoping the public library can help fill in some blanks," Aaron said.

"I'm afraid it's not open today. This is such a small town, they only open twice a week," Linda said. "Not until the day after tomorrow."

"I'll work around it," he said. "There's still more to read in the family papers."

"If you two don't mind, I think I'll go upstairs and take a nap," Linda said. "I seem to be so sleepy these days."

"Tell Linda there's no such thing as a ghost," Dawn begged as soon as she was alone with Aaron.

"There might not be, but I think Linda wants an explanation, not platitudes."

"You put the idea of the house being haunted in her head. Why can't you explain it away?"

"I'll do the best I can. I'm not the ogre you think I am."

Her opinion of him was obvious, not only in her opposition to his investigation, but in the way she tackled the remaining papers on the table with a minimum of conversation. Her dogged but silent work piqued him, but at the same time he was distracted by the strap of her pink tank top. It slid off her shoulder no matter how many times she pushed it back with the tip of one dirty finger, and he wanted to kiss the little knobby bone that made her seem delicate and vulnerable. He wanted to push the narrow strip of cloth back where it belonged himself, but more than that, he wanted to touch her smooth, golden-tanned skin, run his lips over the faint sprinkling of freckles, taste her heated flesh and cool it with the tip of his tongue.

"I'm not accusing you of anything," she said, focusing her eyes on his flattened hand on the surface of the table as he leaned toward her. The back was sun-bronzed with one vein below his knuckles more prominent than the others. If he'd ever worn a wedding ring, the depression on his finger had fleshed out.

"Not of meddling?" He had a boyish whim to impress her, to make her admire him, but the urge to heckle her was even stronger. He wanted to get inside her mind and discover why she was avoiding eye contact.

"It's the big-sister habit," she explained with a half-hearted laugh. "Even before Mom died, I always felt Linda was my responsibility."

"She's a grown-up woman now."

"I know." She did look at him then, a nervous little grin touching her lips then instantly dissolving. "All you have to do is tell her there's no ghost here—nothing paranormal."

"Do you think that would satisfy her?"

"Yes . . . if you give her some kind of explanation."

"I don't have one."

"You could come up with something—a loose branch or . . ."

"An underground stream, a fault in the earth, structural instability in the house . . ."

"Then she'd worry about the house being unsafe."

"Yes, that's why a lie could be worse than looking for the truth."

"Not when she's afraid of something that doesn't exist. You must have some plausible explanation up your sleeve."

"I'm not a magician. What's the real reason you want me to leave?"

He pushed aside his chair and stood so close she felt suffocated by the scent of his warm skin. She could detect the spicy aroma of his cologne under male musk, a heady combination that made her feel jumpy and off balance.

"I'm only concerned with my sister's welfare." She mentally cringed, wondering if she sounded like a semi-hysterical spinster, the kind of woman who would have been walled up in a nunnery in medieval times. With thoughts like that, maybe she should give up reading historical novels.

"Believe it or not, so am I," he said, sounding angry, impatient, and frustrated. "But you're asking me to compromise my integrity by telling Linda soothing lies instead of offering real explanations. Don't you think that could backfire if there really is something paranormal in this house?"

"That's a big if!" She stood and backed away from the table so she could step out of the invisible circle his presence seemed to form around her.

"The best I can do," he said wearily, wondering why the woman drained his energy, "is try not to put ideas in her head. I can't decide on the best course for my investigation until I actually experience what Linda did."

"And to do that, you may have to stay here indefinitely?"

"My time is valuable. I don't waste it on unsubstantiated cases."

"My sister isn't a case! I'm not going to let you prowl around scaring her."

Her sloppy strap was driving him bonkers. Before she could react, he moved closer, slid his finger under it, and put it back where it belonged.

"It was slipping," he said, embarrassed by his gesture but aroused by the warm, silky texture of her skin. "I have work to do."

He turned to go, and she instinctively touched her shoulder, checking the strap, surprised she hadn't given it a thought before he anchored it.

"I'm going to watch everything you do!" It was a reckless, maybe even foolish declaration, and she immediately regretted it.

"Bring a few pillows," he said dryly. "I'm going to keep watch again tonight. Meanwhile, I think I'll have a nap."

When he went upstairs, she felt alone and depressed. It seemed so obvious to her that ghosts couldn't possibly exist, especially not in a pretty old house in rural Wisconsin. The whole situation didn't make sense, and Aaron's presence in her sister's house was the oddest part of the puzzle.

She didn't like the suspicions plaguing her thoughts, but why would a college professor with a successful career be so adamant about investigating this house? Was he trying to make a reputation for himself among paranormal believers?

How far would he go to prove Linda really had had a brush with the occult? She'd read about tricksters faking ghostly sightings at séances, but would Aaron rig some stunt to make it seem the house really was haunted? She didn't doubt he was clever enough to produce the special effects for a one-star horror flick, but was he that determined to prove the house had a spectral visitor?

The worst part was, she didn't want Aaron to be a fraud. But if he planned to deceive her sister, she was the only one who could expose him. Like it or not, she was going to watch with him another night.

Once when she'd been selling at weekend flea markets to survive on her gift-shop salary, Dawn had set up in a small-town high school gym. It had rained continuously all day, a cold, hard, driving deluge that discouraged all but the most die-hard collectors. She'd paid $50 for her space in the gym and sold $27.50 worth of costume jewelry and a $2.00 pair of salt and pepper shakers. She'd counted on the day's receipts to pay her apartment rent. It was three months and four days after the day she didn't get married.

Carrying the last box of unsold merchandise out of the gym, she'd stopped to commiserate over the small number of buyers with a dealer she'd never met before. The woman had been selling the contents of her attic and barn before she and her husband retired to Arkansas. What she hadn't sold, he was going to haul to the dump the next day. A blackened tankard lying in a box with a rotting harness and a plastic dog dish had caught Dawn's eye. She'd offered the woman a dollar for it, and, after ten minutes of haggling, handed over $22.50 leaving her just enough for gas money home. Like many amateurs, the woman had thought everything she was selling was junk until someone wanted it—then it became precious!

After much research, Dawn had learned the tankard was eighteenth-century pewter. It had brought enough at a New York auction to launch her full-time career into antiques and restore her faith in her own instincts—until she met Aaron. She wanted to listen to her instinct now; she wanted to believe he was only there because he wanted to help her sister, but his ghost hunting was too suspicious.

After dinner they played a trivia game, Linda and Dawn against Aaron. He won after he discovered neither of them were good at sports questions.

"I'm going to sleep in my own room tonight," Linda said.

"If you're more comfortable down here..." Dawn suggested, not sure why it made her feel better to have her sister on the lower floor.

"No, I want to get this over with. I have a feeling this thing won't happen again unless I'm upstairs."

Dawn followed her up the steps, urging her to think about her "condition" when Aaron was out of hearing.

"Baby lives in his—or her—little armored tank. I'm not fragile," Linda said, laughing a little too loudly and disagreeing a little too vehemently.

"Well, please do one thing for me," Dawn said, sitting on the edge of Linda's bed. "Loan me a shirt, a big, loose, cool shirt."

"Gary has a few dress shirts that are ready for Goodwill—or whatever people here do with their rummage. Is that what you want?"

"Perfect." Dawn pushed up the strap of her tank top, deciding it needed a tuck before she wore it again.

When Linda was ready for bed, Dawn gathered her supplies for the night's watch: a cooler with a six-pack of cola loaded with caffeine, a stack of pillows from the front porch, and a camping flashlight with a beam bright enough to use as a searchlight for a supermarket opening. She joined Aaron in the storage room an hour after Linda went to bed.

Aaron hid his smile when Dawn came into the room wearing a man's striped dress shirt so large it covered her knees.

"Ready for another night of guarding the dust motes?" she asked, dropping her load of pillows on the blanket he'd already spread on the floor. "You've moved things around."

"I wanted to see what was stored in the back. It turned out to be a bigger job than I expected."

"Linda and Gary will get around to it when they have time."

"I'm not treasure hunting," he said, annoyed by her unspoken accusation.

"If tonight is a bust, will you give up and leave?" She made a big production out of arranging the pillows in a cozy nest for one.

He watched silently as she plumped and pummeled the pillows, acting as agitated as he felt.

"Well, will you?" she challenged.

"This investigation really disturbs you, doesn't it?"

His sympathetic tone only made her angry. "Of course it does. This isn't good for Linda, thinking there's something unearthly in her own home."

"Your work is pretty flexible, isn't it?" he asked, unwrapping a cellophane-covered hard candy and offering it to her.

She shook her head to refuse it. "Not really. Either Jane or I have to be at the mall most of the time. Jane's husband, Derek, is helping evenings and weekends while I'm gone."

"What I mean is, could you take your vacation a few weeks from now? Maybe you'd be happier if you left tomorrow and came back later."

"Me go instead of you?"

"I think I could resolve the situation more quickly." He sounded pompous and hated it. "You're a distraction, Dawn."

"Why am I a distraction?" She sucked in her breath, then sneezed violently when dust tickled her nostrils. "Someone has to look after my sister's interests."

"I stirred up a lot of dust today," he said apologetically. "At least I managed to open the back window partway."

"Don't avoid my question. Why do you want me to go?"

He didn't know how to answer without revealing more of his feelings than he wanted to. Dawn was a distraction because he loved the sound of her voice, the softness of her skin, the golden glints in her hair. When she was around, he wasn't giving one hundred percent to the investigation. This wasn't a situation he welcomed; he wasn't ready for commitment or for any relationship that would be emotionally satisfying to a woman.

"I don't exactly want you to go," he hedged, not wanting to hurt her feelings or arouse more suspicions about the investigation. "I'm only warning you that most of what I do is pretty dull, dry stuff. It can't be fun for you to sit in the dark all night with nothing to do but struggle to stay awake. It's not anyone's idea of a good vacation."

"Isn't this your vacation?"

"I'm not teaching any courses this summer, but I think of this as work."

"I've always made it my job to look out for Linda. She's the only family I have."

"Believe me, I won't do anything to hurt Linda."

"How can I be sure of that?"

Below them, Lucky howled, adding his protests to hers, and Dawn wiggled until the pillows separated and left her hipbone in contact with a floorboard.

"The rocker is pretty comfortable," he suggested mildly, "unless you've changed your mind about staying here all night."

"I haven't."

She stood and stared at the mission oak chair. The leather seat was worn and sagging, but the brown-stained wood seemed as sturdy as when it had left the factory early in the century. Trying to visualize it in the downstairs parlor, she felt vague tingles trailing down her spine. "Imagine if furniture could talk," she said, hugging herself with a shudder.

"There's a theory that inanimate objects absorb emotional energy," he said.

"Does that mean ghosts are only replays of traumatic experiences, like horror videos without the necessity of using a machine to view them?"

"I've never thought of it quite that way." He laughed softly, amused as she stubbornly tried again to get comfortable on the floor. "You know a little more about the paranormal than you've let on."

"Everyone reads the tabloids in the grocery line." She watched him drop down on his knees beside her.

"Elvis's Ghost Predicts Grammy Awards," he joked.

"Ghost Fathers Siamese Twins."

"Elvis's Ghost Haunts Kalamazoo Drive-in."

"How seriously do you take this?" she asked, impulsively picking up the flashlight and activating the beam so it hit him squarely in the face.

He shaded his eyes and reached out to grab the long aluminum cylinder. "What do you call this, the third degree?"

"That's right, tough guy. You'd better spill the beans." She did her best tough-cop imitation and held on to the flashlight.

He clicked off the light, covering her hand with his. It was small and soft, fitting into his palm as though it belonged there. His heart gave an odd lurch, and he didn't want her to be his adversary.

"Something's happening here," he said so softly she had to strain to hear him. "Something neither of us is ready to deal with."

"No." She didn't believe her own denial.

"Wanting me to leave . . . is it only because of Linda?"

"I don't like to see her scared."

"Is there anything else you're afraid of?"

He explored her fingers with his thumb, tracing the outlines of her nails and caressing each knuckle in turn.

"Spiders—definitely spiders. And I'd just as soon snakes kept out of my way, too." She tried to pull her hand away.

"Dawn, it's not a good idea for you to wait here in the dark with me."

She glanced at the scanty light coming through the open doorway from the hall and realized her lower lip was trembling. Biting down hard to stop it, she didn't know whether to blame his shivery voice, her own longings, or the intensity of being together in the storage room. For once she agreed with him, but it was beyond her powers to get up and walk away from him.

"You're scaring me," she said, aware that she was taking the easy way out in blaming him. What scared her were the feelings he aroused in her.

"I don't mean to." He leaned closer, still on his knees, with her hand securely enclosed in his. "Don't fight whatever it is you're sensing. Share it with me."

"There's nothing to share," she said emphatically, trying to convince herself as well as him. "This room is giving me the creeps. That's all."

"Go to bed."

"No."

"I'm afraid..."

"Not you?"

"I'm afraid I'm going to kiss you again."

"That's a terrible idea."

"Is it?"

His face was so close his breath tickled her chin.

"I've never kissed a man with a beard before..."

"If you say things like that, I may take them as challenges."

"No, don't." She protested so weakly that it sounded like an invitation.

Her lips parted expectantly, but he only rubbed his nose against hers, his breath warm and teasing.

"That tickles."

He slid his free hand around her back, feeling nothing but smooth skin and the hard ridge of her spine under the oversize shirt. He remembered the pink strap slipping off her shoulder and moved his mouth against hers.

His first kiss was feathery light, toying with her lips and parting them with the tip of his tongue. She waited breathlessly, letting her hands rest lightly on the hard bulges of his biceps, then sliding them behind his neck to stroke the soft, wavy hair clustered there.

Don't start this, he warned himself, but he didn't want anything to do with logic or practicalities. He'd put his emotions on a back burner too long; they were boiling over now, and he didn't want to consider the consequences.

"I like you," he whispered.

A declaration of love would have shocked her into backing away from him; she only smiled at his boyish endearment, not prepared for a kiss that made her tingle all the way to her toes.

Throwing caution aside, she kissed him back, wrapping her arms around him and spreading her fingers on his back. Her breath was trapped in her chest, and she felt giddy, a light-headedness that made her vulnerable to a sudden overriding stab of fear. Panicking, she tried to push him away but didn't know why. Her senses went berserk: her ears felt plugged, but she heard keening inside her head; her nostrils filled with a musty odor; pinpricks of light danced inside her closed lids.

"Dawn!" His voice came from a million light-years away, and the floor seemed to be sinking under her.

A sudden shrill, piercing scream pulled her back from the edge of a black abyss, and she realized she'd been on the verge of fainting.

"Linda!" She screamed her sister's name and leaned on Aaron to stagger to her feet. He was faster than she was, pulling her along behind him as they raced toward the bedroom.

Chapter Four

Linda's screams sent ripples of terror through Dawn. She pushed past Aaron and reached the bedroom first, nearly colliding with her sister in the open doorway.

"What's wrong?" She instinctively hugged her, more frightened than she'd been since that terrible moment years ago in the drugstore when she'd returned from her scooter ride to find her little sister gone.

"The vibrations..."

"Calm down, Linda. You're all right." Aaron spoke with quiet assurance, and Linda pulled away from Dawn and went to him.

"You must have felt them...?"

"Let's go downstairs and talk this over," he suggested.

Dawn watched dumbfounded as Linda docilely followed him down the stairs. One minute she was hysterical and the next she was like damp clay in the ghost hunter's hands. Instead of being relieved, Dawn was more worried than ever. Was Aaron manipulating her sister for some reason of his own? She had a terrible vision of a mad scientist using mind control to lure his victim to... to what?

Her cheeks were burning, and she could still feel the tingle of his touch against her skin. Maybe lack of oxygen in the stuffy storage room had made her semi-intoxicated. Or could she have had an allergic reaction to dust that had befuddled her senses? There had to be some excuse—some reason—for her reaction to Aaron. She couldn't be attracted to a man who was throwing her sister's life into chaos with his wild ghost chase.

Guilty and confused, she hurried after them, finding them in the kitchen where Aaron was pouring two glasses of milk.

"Would you like some?" he asked Dawn.

"No." She found one of the heavy white mugs and filled it with tap water, gulping it down to quench her raging thirst. Maybe she'd been drugged! There had to be some explanation for the effect Aaron had on her. But she was afraid it was much more complicated than that.

"Please, don't keep me in suspense," Linda pleaded. "You did feel it, didn't you?"

Aaron sat beside her, his back toward Dawn, who was still standing by the sink.

"I can't—I won't—lie to you. I didn't experience the phenomenon."

"Neither did I," Dawn said, although she had a strong feeling neither of them wanted to hear from her.

"Describe exactly what happened," Aaron said in his low, soothing, professional voice.

Much as she distrusted him, Dawn couldn't help but see how calm Linda was when she started to tell her story.

"I was sound asleep. I know I wasn't having a nightmare. Then suddenly I was wide awake. It was the same noise—a rhythmic sound—in the hall right outside my room. Then the door started to open by itself. I know it was closed when I went to sleep. I wouldn't sleep with it open when I have guests."

Dawn didn't like being included as a "guest," and she didn't like being lumped in with the ghost hunter. She was family, not a visitor.

"How long did the phenomenon last?" Aaron asked.

"I'm not sure. It seemed to go on and on. At first I was too frightened to scream."

"Let's talk about the nature of the sound."

"You're sure you didn't hear anything?" Linda looked ready to cry. "Dawn, did you?"

"Sorry, no." She wanted to offer more comfort, but Linda wouldn't like any explanation she could suggest: nightmare, thumping dog tail, a squirrel on the roof.

"You said the sound was rhythmic," Aaron went on. "Did it remind you of a marching band—not the music, but the sound of feet on pavement during a lull in a parade?"

"That's a hard question."

That's a ridiculous question, Dawn wanted to say, but she felt totally left out of their conversation. Sheer stubbornness made her stay while Aaron had her sister go over and over the alleged experience.

When he finally relented and agreed with Linda that she finish the night on the air mattress downstairs, Dawn felt useless. She went to her own bedroom as soon as she was sure there was nothing Linda wanted her to do.

She crawled into bed, wishing she didn't feel obligated to stay there. Thinking about the paranormal was like grappling with an object made of molasses. It was sticky and messy, changing shape and dissolving under close scrutiny. She liked to tackle concrete problems with clear-cut solutions.

Later, but probably not hours later as it seemed, she heard Aaron's door close. Tossing and turning, sleepless in the ornately carved antique bed, she finally had a revelation.

"Dr. Ghostbuster" had left his small recorder on the dining-room table. He hadn't taped a single word of Linda's spooky experience. Dawn didn't know whether to be more or less worried at his lapse. Wasn't this "case" interesting enough to record, or was he so interested in Linda's reaction that he forgot about it? Why was he so determined to stay?

The smell of bacon woke her, and Dawn hurried down-stairs in her short, rosy-red velour robe, eager to see how her sister was.

"How was the rest of your night?" she began, rushing into the kitchen.

"It was one I won't forget in a hurry." Aaron was stand-ing by the stove in a pair of sweats that hugged his round, firm bottom and a gray shirt that left his lean, tanned mid-section exposed. She wasn't surprised when he turned around and she could read the logo: Stolen from UW Ath-letic Dept.

"Did you really steal it?"

"What?"

"The shirt."

"No, just typical collegiate humor. How do you like your eggs?"

There was something so cozy about a man cooking breakfast that she had to suppress an urge to rumple his hair.

Annoyed at herself for letting him inside her head, she made a lame excuse about not being ready for breakfast and went back upstairs.

When she came down again, showered and dressed in a long denim skirt and a blue oxford-cloth shirt with rolled-up sleeves, she found only Linda in the kitchen.

"Um, you're all dressed up," her sister said, just finish-ing a bite of blueberry muffin. "Sorry we didn't wait breakfast for you. Aaron said you came down and went back up. I thought we'd go to an auction this morning, but you'll have to eat and change in a hurry if you want time to look things over before the bidding starts."

"How are you?" Dawn asked, a little surprised by her sister's chipper mood.

"Fine now that I've had a good breakfast. Eating seems to settle my stomach in the morning."

"About last night..."

"I've gone over and over it with Aaron. He knows I didn't imagine it, but he doesn't think there's any reason to be afraid."

"Where is he?" Her sister's happy mood eased her worries, but talking about the ghost hunter made her feel decidedly sour.

"Oh, he wanted to do a few things before we leave for the auction. Just like a man to cook and run. Gary never even considers cleaning up after he plays chef. I saved you some bacon."

"No, thanks. You can save it to crumble on a salad later. I'll just have toast and coffee."

"Okay. If you didn't bring enough shorts, you're welcome to borrow a pair from me. They won't fit me pretty soon anyway."

"No, I'll just wear what I have on, thanks." She couldn't explain why she wanted to feel as covered up as possible, regardless of how warm it might become that day.

Dawn drove, following Linda's complicated directions to reach an aging two-story farmhouse with peeling white paint. She'd rejected Aaron's offer to drive either his Jeep Cherokee or her van. Laudable or not, she needed to feel in control of something in this bizarre visit to her sister's home.

Linda talked all the way, but she didn't sound like herself. Was she pretending to be happy to cover a deeper fear about her odd dreams than she'd admit? Or was she blos-

soming under Aaron's concern? Dawn knew her sister loved
Gary madly and without reservations, but Linda was actually glowing with enthusiasm as she monopolized the ghost
hunter's attention.

That part was fine with Dawn, but she wanted him to
leave more than ever. Linda was hearing things inside her
own head, and Dawn was deeply alarmed for her sake. She
loved her sister dearly, but she didn't understand how they
could be so totally different. Linda needed a man to lean on.
Dawn took pride in her independence and self-sufficiency;
she didn't plan to depend on anyone, especially not a man
who hunted ghosts as a hobby.

Aaron enjoyed an occasional country auction, but there
were too many unanswered questions back at the Hall home.
He'd wanted to stay behind to see if anyone would let him
into the library before it opened tomorrow—sometimes academic credentials could open doors—but Linda was worrying him. She was too cheerful—almost giddy—and she
seemed to be blocking the terror out of her mind instead of
facing it. He was missing something important in working
with her, and he didn't want to let her out of his sight just
yet.

He signed up for a bidding number when the two women
got theirs, amazed by the casual way things were done in this
rural area. He didn't even need to show his driver's license
to get a bid card. Too bad his dealings with Dawn weren't
so simple. She was angry—or at least upset with him—and
overprotective of her sister.

"Are you looking for anything special?" he asked Dawn
as the three of them wandered around looking at the clutter
spread out on a long double row of tables set up on the
lawn.

"I'm always looking for resale merchandise." With sunglasses and a wide-brimmed straw hat pulled low on her

forehead, she was hiding as much of herself as possible on a bright, sunny day.

"That's a nice group of old radios," he said, making small talk as he followed them along a row of furniture that included a chrome and Formica-topped kitchen table and a platform rocker with springs poking through the upholstery on the seat.

"Not one of my specialties," she said dismissively.

"I don't suppose they work," he said to both women. "That chair is nice."

Dawn looked at him, parting her lips a little as though his good taste surprised her. "Balloon back, walnut, nice sharp carving." She walked around it, taking off her sunglasses for a better look. "Unfortunately, it's been repaired."

He saw the messy glue job on the back and nodded sagely, stifling an urge to pretend to be more knowledgeable about antiques than he was. Her opinion of him had dipped lower than a thermometer in the Arctic—not that it had been very high to begin with.

What was even harder to understand was why he cared. She was beautiful—that he had to admit. He had to give her high marks on intelligence and independence, too, attributes he admired in a woman, but he knew dozens of female instructors at the university who were loaded with brains and initiative. None of them attracted him right now; he was getting used to living alone, and for now, it was right for him. Not that a bevy of faculty wives would ever accept his solitary status; he was on the blind-date list of every female married to one of his colleagues.

"There's a table of toys and games by the house," Dawn said, not exactly issuing him an invitation to look it over with her. He followed, anyway, putting his hand protectively on Linda's shoulder, wondering why she was so quiet now. Was she deferring to her sister's greater knowledge of antiques, or was her false sense of well-being wearing off?

"We can't keep enough old toys stocked in the mall," Dawn said, picking up a chicken pull-toy and examining it critically. "This is cute, paper on wood, but I do best with toys for big boys—metal cars, wind-ups, anything space related."

"Space?"

"Not antique, I know, but some Star Wars and Star Trek collectibles are worth their weight in gold. Old tin robots made in Japan are out-of-sight too."

"Worth hundreds?" he asked, more interested in thawing the ice between them than in speculating in old toys.

"Thousands." She lifted the cover on a faded old Lotto box. "Not complete. This is nice though."

He looked skeptically at a faded rubber Mickey Mouse in a little car. He couldn't see the value in sandbox castoffs, but then, she didn't have much use for his psychic investigations.

The auctioneer was vintage cornball in a cowboy hat and alligator boots, but once he got past the chitchat and jokes, he sold skillfully and fast, starting high, quickly dropping if he didn't get an immediate opening bid, then urging the crowd back to the price he was looking for on many of the lots.

Linda bought a box of what looked like old pot holders and dish towels, then triumphantly showed her sister a piece of lace.

"Belgian?" she asked.

"Yes, and handmade. You should start your own shop up here," Dawn said.

"Then I'd have to sell all my beautiful finds."

Dawn let the Mickey Mouse go to a huge-bellied man in overalls at a price that made Aaron whistle through his teeth, but she bought a jar of broken costume jewelry.

"Loaded with rhinestone," she explained. "Jane's husband is good at repairing the better pieces."

She also bought an album of old postcards—not batting an eye at a hundred and twenty dollars—and a milk-glass bowl with little flowers painted on it.

Aaron bought a box of pinback buttons with slogans from the sixties: Make Love Not War, War Is Hazardous To Children And Other Living Things. He thought he'd stick them on his bulletin board to lure a student or two into absorbing a little history.

"Not what I'd expect to find at a farm auction," he mused.

"Anything can turn up," Linda said. "That's what makes it so much fun."

"That and the dream of buying a thousand-dollar antique with a two-dollar bid," Dawn said.

Aaron laughed, but Linda protested, "You always think of the price of things."

"Are you saying I'm materialistic?" Dawn sounded genuinely hurt.

"No, I didn't mean it that way. Only that you're on top of things—you have to know values to be a dealer."

The sisters were quickly reconciled, but Aaron was puzzled by his own reaction to their flare-up. Linda often came across as charming and defenseless, but he'd had an irrational urge to leap to Dawn's defense, sure that she cared deeply about people, especially her sister.

While the auctioneer worked his way through an enormous pile of tools, Aaron walked over and stared morosely at one of the vintage radios still waiting to be sold. It was a floor model with frayed cloth over the speaker, a missing knob, and warped veneer on the top.

"Nineteen thirties," Dawn said, coming up beside him. "Imagine what it could tell us if objects could store emanations from the past."

She'd voiced his own thoughts, and he was stunned by the emotional impact she had on him.

"I always wonder who owned the antiques that go through my hands, what kind of people they were, whether they had happy or sad lives. When a piece is battered and dirty, I blame it on bad things happening to the people who owned it. People who love life are more likely to cherish their possessions for the memories they hold." She laughed self-consciously. "That's my theory, anyway."

"Is that what nostalgia is? I guess that explains why people want to collect the same toys they played with as children. Maybe there's a lesson for psychologists here," he mused.

"What's that?"

"To pay more attention to the types of things people value. Maybe there's material for an article on why people collect old toys."

"Maybe." She remembered the sunglasses she'd been dangling between her fingers and put them on. "But I don't believe a piece of furniture can be haunted, like an old radio that keeps replaying programs that were aired years ago."

"It's only a theory," he said mildly, watching as her hair whipped out from under the brim of her straw hat in a breeze that made her skirt billow out like a ship's sail.

"It's going to rain. I guess we should pay and go," she said, abruptly changing her mood.

He looked up, surprised to see dark clouds vying with the sun for possession of the sky.

"I enjoyed today," he said, trying to recapture the accord between them.

"I did too. It was fun," she said quietly.

Aaron and Dawn said little on the way home; the silence was broken only by Linda's speculation about her Belgian lace.

"How do you suppose handmade lace ended up in a Wisconsin farm sale?" she asked.

"Servicemen brought home a lot of souvenirs after World War II...and World War I," Dawn suggested.

"I'm going to frame it with a black background, I think. Of course, I'll have to find something that won't stain the lace."

"Sounds nice," her sister said absentmindedly.

"I thought you might be able to suggest something I can use."

"I'll think about it," Dawn promised, her mind too full of confusing thoughts about Aaron to concentrate on anything else.

He had an appealing curiosity about everything, and there seemed to be little that didn't interest him. He was sitting behind her, the postcard album on his lap, studying each era card inserted into slits in the black sugar-paper pages.

"Maybe I'll wear it instead," Linda said, oblivious to the preoccupied silence of the other two. "There's not enough for a shawl, but maybe I can make a collar. Or would that ruin it?"

"You'll think of something," Dawn said, sorry she couldn't share her sister's enthusiasm over a very nice find.

Big drops splattered the windshield as they pulled into the Hall's driveway, and they had to race for the porch to avoid getting soaked. Aaron held the door for the two women, then followed them inside with the shoulders of his shirt darkened by rain.

"I'll be upstairs if you want me," he said, eager to get back to his reason for being there.

Linda decided to nap on the air mattress downstairs, but Dawn was too agitated to rest. She looked through her jar of broken jewelry, pleased to find several marked pieces that needed only minor repairs. The postcard album was an even better buy. Among several hundred old views and greetings were a dozen Halloween cards that would be easy to sell and more than repay her investment. Any other time she would have started removing the better cards and penciling prices in small, neat numerals on the address sides, but she was too worried to concentrate.

Linda wasn't herself today, but was it pregnancy or fear that made her work so hard at sounding cheerful? Dawn thought of calling Linda's doctor, but her sister wouldn't appreciate her interference. Also, it was doubtful whether a physician who'd only seen her once could offer much help.

One person could help—by leaving. The prospect of confronting Aaron and again asking him to go made her even more gloomy. She sat on the living room couch and watched raindrops cascade down a window obscuring the gray vista beyond the pane of glass.

Dawn fixed dinner, a big salad with crumbled bits of bacon and cheese and freshly baked corn muffins from a mix she found in the cupboard. She woke Linda at seven o'clock p.m., then called up the stairs to Aaron.

They ate in front of the TV in the den like kids clustered around a cartoon show, avoiding conversation as they watched an old movie. The hero of the dated film had a gift that allowed him to bring a statue to life; Dawn couldn't help thinking of Aaron's kiss, remembering how vibrant and alive it had made her feel.

Much to her sister's relief, Linda decided to sleep downstairs that night. They parted for bed after a halfhearted game of Monopoly that Linda won by refusing to buy any property until she landed on Park Place and Boardwalk. Dawn wound up with mortgaged utilities and two get-out-of-jail-free cards.

"If you don't mind, I'll spend the night in the master bedroom, Linda," Aaron said.

"I'd be so grateful if you would."

He glanced in Dawn's direction, but she didn't know if he expected approval or an argument from her.

"I'll be awake and watching, too," she assured her sister. "You get as much sleep as you can."

She'd spoken to reassure her sister, but the prospect of another night alone with Aaron was daunting. She'd gone beyond mistrusting him; she didn't trust herself not to respond to his searing kisses. How could she be an impartial watchdog when she was so vulnerable to his sexy charm?

Aaron moved his recording equipment into the master bedroom, put his thermos of coffee on the nightstand, took off his shoes, and stretched out on a sheet he'd put on top of the bed. He was too grubby from shifting all his equipment to lie on her pale-blue-and-white quilted spread, but his body rebelled at the thought of another night on the floor.

He was tired, but listening to every night sound inside and outside the house kept him alert. The luminous numbers on the bedside clock showed 11:20 when he finally heard a telltale creak on one of the polished wooden steps.

Dawn was coming, but would she go to her room or keep her promise to her sister and watch with him? He ached in anticipation, beginning to doubt his own motives for staying in the house. Even before he saw her silhouetted in the open doorway, the yellow light of the hallway behind her, he imagined the slender curve of her waist, the tantalizing fullness of her breasts, and her tawny hair flowing down to her shoulders.

She peeked into her sister's room, hoping he'd succumbed to sleep. She couldn't keep her promise to Linda in her own room, but she could hope he wasn't awake.

A floorboard squeaked loudly, hardly muffled at all by the old carpeting, and she felt as if she'd been caught doing something sneaky.

"Come in," he invited, flicking on a small lamp on the nightstand.

"I just wanted to know whether you're awake. Linda's depending on you...why, I don't know!"

It suddenly seemed so urgent that she share the watch with him; he was afraid to ask if she was going to.

"You still think this is all a charade, don't you?" he asked.

"Do you honestly believe Linda heard ghosts frolicking in the hallway?" She took one step into the room, as wary as a hiker approaching quicksand.

"I don't formulate beliefs about phenomena like that. I only wait and observe."

"There's nothing to observe."

"Not yet."

"But you expect to see or hear something?"

"All I hope to do is put Linda's mind at ease."

"You didn't record her story the other night."

"You wouldn't want me to write about this case, would you? I don't need notes to go on for Linda's sake." He also had a feeling that he'd never forget the memorable details of being in the house with Dawn.

"Thank you...for that," she said grudgingly. "But Linda will be fine. There's no reason to stay longer."

"Isn't there?"

His voice was soft and challenging, making her spine tingle and her breath catch in her throat.

"No, I don't think so."

He put his legs over the side of the bed, then stood, his hair an unruly mane since the rain had dampened it.

"Linda sensed something," he said automatically, unable to concentrate on anything but the way Dawn's lips puckered in disapproval and her eyes narrowed with doubt.

"It's all in her head." Even as she said it, she didn't want it to be true. She wanted her sister's mind to be healthy and strong.

"Maybe." He heard the drumming of his heart as he thought about holding Dawn in his arms. "The only way to be sure is to experience it myself. I still may, if there's a stronger manifestation. Linda is probably more sensitive than I am. Are you going to trust my report in the morning?"

He'd hooked her in the only way possible. If she went to her own room, she would have to worry about whether he'd fill Linda's head with make-believe happenings in the morning.

"If you hear anything, I'll hear it from my room," she said.

"So far, Linda only experienced the phenomenon when she was in this room."

Dawn moistened her lips with the tip of her tongue, angry because she'd allowed a disturbing vision to pop into her head: the two of them intertwined on her sister's bed, their lips locked together, his hands moving on her back...

"Then I'll have to stay here," she reluctantly decided.

He read her anger correctly: she was mad at herself for wanting to be with him. He felt like a man who'd just received a gift-wrapped package but was afraid to open it. The contents could be terribly disappointing, but he'd never know unless he took the risk.

"Come in." His voice seemed to be coming from far away, and he swallowed hard, his eyes out of focus as she slowly moved closer to the bed.

She glanced around the room, momentarily miffed with her sister for not including a single chair among the room's furnishings, not even one of the nondescript metal folding chairs. Then she spotted the window seat lost in the shadow at the back of the room.

"I'll sit here," she said in a husky voice that didn't seem to belong to her.

He was disappointed, even though the sane, rational side of his mind knew she wouldn't cuddle with him on the bed.

"Suit yourself," he said gruffly, stretching out flat with pillows behind his head. He would be more comfortable than she was . . . or would he?

Had she been sitting on the hard window seat for an hour? Two hours? Dawn's backside was numb, and she resented Aaron's obvious comfort, even though she couldn't actually see his form sprawled on the bed. He'd turned off the small bedside light and partly closed the door, so only a feeble shaft of light sliced into the thick darkness of the room. The rain had slowed to a monotonous drip, drip, drip that set her teeth on edge.

As though reading her mind, he proved he was still awake. "You can't be very comfortable there. This is a queen-size bed. If you want to lie down, I'll pretend there's an invisible wall down the middle."

"I'm fine here."

"No, you're not." He got up and walked over to her, sitting down on the window seat.

His thigh was crowding hers, and his shoulder was so close she had to shrink away to avoid pressing against it.

"This seat isn't big enough for both of us," she protested.

"The bed is." He deliberately moved closer, torturing himself by pressing against her soft, smooth thigh.

"I don't believe in invisible things, especially not walls."

"Air is invisible, it keeps us alive."

"So are germs, ragweed pollen, and viruses."

"You have my word. Come lie down. It won't matter if you doze off. The phenomena seems to start when Linda's deeply asleep."

He took her hand and pulled her to her feet, his palm firm and strong, exerting just enough pressure to make him seem protective.

The bed did feel wonderful. He handed her one of Linda's plump pillows, then moved to the far edge, keeping his promise not to touch her.

The steady beat of rain on the roof was the only sound. She curled up on her side and surrendered to fatigue.

His nose tickled, and he reached out, more asleep than awake, to brush away the silky tendril that was causing it.

I'm in trouble, he thought groggily, trying to move away only to find his leg pinned to the bed. The room was gray with the light of early morning, and he could see the cascade of hair spreading across the pillow beside him. He didn't remember moving to take her in his arms, but he couldn't deny that it felt right for her to be there.

At least she was still asleep. As gently as possible, he tried to inch his leg out from under hers, but every time he moved, she stirred.

"Did you hear anything?" she murmured sleepily, and he froze, feigning sleep in an attempt to establish his innocence.

Her breathing became regular again, but she was pressed against him spoon-fashion, her back against his front. He put his arm around her, inhaling the perfume of her hair, surprised at how warm and protective she made him feel. Amazingly, he felt a sleepy contentment that had eluded him for many long months.

The room was sunny when she woke up, but it took her a minute to realize why she felt so warm and secure. Aaron was stretched out beside her, strands of her hair trapped under his cheek.

So much for invisible walls, she ruefully thought, then realized she could see a broad expanse of bed from where she lay. He wasn't on her side; she was on his!

Hoping against hope that he'd never know it, she tried to roll away, but there was no way to free her trapped hair.

"Aaron, let me up," she whispered, hoping to be gone before he realized what had happened.

"Mmm." He lifted his head and smiled, releasing her hair but reaching out to take her in his arms. "Good morning, darling," he murmured in the drowsy state between dreaming and wakefulness. When he realized what he'd said, he felt too happy to regret it.

His eyes were shut, and dark hair was covering his forehead in unruly waves. He rose up on one elbow and trailed his lips over her cheek, then nuzzled the wildly seductive spot under her ear. When he bent to sample her lips, she started to remember all the reasons to keep away from him, but by then it was too late to resist his tender kiss. His tongue parted her lips, and she locked her mouth against his, letting waves of sensation radiate through her body.

His tongue swelled to fill her, and she reached out to touch him, making contact with his bare midsection under the cut-off athletic shirt. She loved the feel of his warm, taut skin, but worry nagged at the fringe of her consciousness.

Was Linda all right? It was morning, and her guardians were too distracted to know if she was safe.

"We have to—" she began, her words cut off by a long, sweet kiss that made her tremble with weakness.

"I'm sorry about the wall," he murmured.

"Linda," she gasped, her lips soft and swollen.

"Linda," he groaned, reluctantly letting responsibility do what the invisible wall had failed to do: separate them.

He sat up, then slowly smiled. "You're on my side."

"Accidentally!" She tried to get up but he pulled her back, pinning her down and hovering over her.

"You knew where to find me," he teased, wishing he could turn back the clock for a few minutes and lose himself in her warm, promising kisses.

"No, I didn't. Not purposely."

She squirmed and he let her go, his soft laughter following her across the room.

"I'm used to having a whole bed to myself," she alibied.

She hurried down to check on Linda.

"Are you all right?"

"Fine. Did you sleep in your clothes?" Linda asked.

Dawn looked down at her wrinkled blouse and skirt, still at a loss to understand why she'd awakened in Aaron's arms.

"It was too late to bother undressing," she said, hoping her sister would buy such a weak excuse.

"Did you hear anything at all?" For once Linda didn't try to disguise her anxiety, and Dawn felt wretched for not taking her sister's experiences more seriously when they happened. Maybe they weren't dreams. It wasn't like Linda to be afraid of something no one else could hear, but there was no doubt about her state of mind. She was terrified.

"I'm sorry," Dawn said, putting her arm around Linda's shoulders. "You can ask Aaron, but I didn't hear a thing."

She escaped as quickly as possible, miserable in the face of Linda's fear and her own inability to help her sister.

The shower was free when she went to use it, but the air in the room was warm and moist. She could feel damp spots on the bath mat where Aaron had stepped only minutes earlier, and the room was fragrant with spicy men's cologne.

Quickly stripping, she turned on the shower full-blast and let the water cascade down on her head, as though she could wash away all the disturbing thoughts crowding her mind.

Aaron sat on the edge of the bed in his briefs, one sock on and his foot poised to pull on the other, but he wasn't in a hurry to dress and go downstairs. He needed to do some hard thinking, but when Dawn was around, his brain turned to mush.

What the hell was happening in this house? Was he dealing with a hysterical female or a puzzling paranormal manifestation? In most cases, his background in psychology and his experience with the paranormal would have pointed him in the right direction by now. Here he didn't have a firm plan for bringing his investigation to a conclusion, and the fault was all his. He had one thing on his mind, and it wasn't ghost hunting.

The memory of holding Dawn was bittersweet. She was the first woman since his divorce to really get under his skin, but he wasn't ready for entanglements or commitments. He wanted to forget her and get on with his investigation, but underneath her mistrust and defensiveness, there was a compelling quality he couldn't begin to define.

"Psychologists are all nuts," he said, lumping himself with the occasional oddball in his profession, but he knew there was more to his feeling for Dawn than middle-aged lust.

He finally finished dressing and decided to skip breakfast. He had a problem to solve, and Linda was a sweet kid. He wanted to put her mind at ease.

He couldn't walk away from his growing attraction to Dawn until he'd figured out what was terrifying her sister.

Chapter Five

Aaron became the invisible man, leaving Dawn alone with her sister until Linda left for a late-morning hair appointment. Dawn was happy for a chance to talk babies, and it should have been the happiest of visits, sharing the excitement and anticipation of a new life. Unfortunately an air of restrained politeness permeated the house. Dawn still believed the "ghost" was somehow inside her sister's head, but she was reluctant to express opinions her sister might resent.

Instead of talking it out as they usually did when they had differences, they avoided the subject. Dawn didn't want to upset Linda; Linda didn't seem to want to face Dawn's skepticism. They didn't mention Aaron at all. Did Linda suspect the attraction between her sister and the ghost hunter?

After Linda had left, Dawn thought of a dozen things she should have said to break the ice between them. As adults, they'd always been good friends as well as siblings. Their friendship was strained, and Dawn felt terrible about it. She missed their closeness.

The phone rang, sounding shrill in the quiet old kitchen where Dawn had been reading the auction classifieds in the Milwaukee *Sentinel*, delivered each morning by car.

"Hall residence," she said, welcoming any distraction.

"Linda?"

"No, this is her sister. She should be back in an hour or so."

"Dawn, I'm so glad you're there. It's Gary."

"Are you calling from Japan?"

"'Fraid so. What are the two of you up to?" Her brother-in-law's voice boomed out of the receiver, as hearty and assertive as if he were in the same room.

What aren't we up to? Dawn wanted to say, feeling like a modern-day Pandora sitting on a chestful of secrets.

"We went to an auction. Linda found a piece of handmade lace in a box with some grubby linens."

"Nice," he said politely. "Where is my girl?"

"Getting her hair done."

"Tell her I called, and I should be able to phone again in about an hour. No, better make that two hours."

"I'm sure she'll be back before then. I'll tell her you're going to call."

"Nice talking to you, Dawn."

The phone went dead in her ear, and Dawn wondered if she'd done Linda a favor by not mentioning her weird experiences. Even if Gary thought Dawn was exaggerating, he was crazy about her sister. He might be able to talk her out of imaginary fears. But he wouldn't understand about Aaron. Also, she couldn't tell him the whole story without mentioning the pregnancy, and that would rob Linda of the supreme joy of telling him herself. Guilty as Dawn felt, she couldn't betray her sister's trust by telling Gary what was happening.

She sat at the table again, staring at the newspaper for several minutes before realizing she'd read the same auction notice three times without absorbing a word.

Aaron hadn't come down for breakfast, and only an occasional thump or scraping noise from the storage room above the kitchen indicated he was still in the house. She felt delinquent in her duty, not watching what he was doing. This might be the best opportunity she'd have all day to speak to him alone, but she couldn't make herself go up the stairs to confront him. She had been on his side of the bed!

"How do you like it?" Linda asked, bursting into the kitchen while Dawn was still poring through the morning paper. "I had it cut."

"Cute. I like it shorter."

"I want to try some easy styles before the baby comes. I won't have time to fuss with my hair when there's a newborn in the house."

"Good news—Gary called."

"Oh, no! I would miss him! How is he? Did he say when he's coming home?"

"I didn't want to ask a lot of questions. It must cost a fortune to call from Japan. He said he'd try again in a few hours." She didn't want to be as specific as Gary had been in case he disappointed Linda.

"I'll stay glued to the phone until he does. I hope it's this afternoon. I was invited to a needlecraft group this evening. I thought I'd take my lace along and see if anyone has any suggestions. You can come, too, if you like. I only know the woman who invited me, but it's at her house. She was having her hair done, too. She said to be sure to invite you. Exactly when did Gary call?"

Dawn told her, glad her sister had had a chance to meet more people.

"Of course, I won't leave the house until Gary calls," Linda said, sounding more like her normal self.

"I think I'll pass on the meeting," Dawn said. "I'm really not much into crafts."

"You don't mind if I go?"

"No, I want you to get acquainted as quickly as possible. You'll enjoy your new home more when you have a circle of friends."

Gary's call and the prospect of an evening out seemed to work miracles on Linda's mood. Dawn was more convinced than ever that Aaron should pack up his ghost hunting equipment and fade away into the mist.

He didn't come down for lunch.

"Aaron told me not to bother about him," Linda explained, jumping to another subject before Dawn could ask any questions.

After eating, they looked through catalogs, making a list of baby things Linda would need.

"You'll have showers," Dawn warned. "I've bought enough baby gifts for friends to dress quints for a year."

"You'll have your turn," Linda promised. "You're so pretty and..."

"I'm not holding my breath." Dawn's tone was friendly, but she didn't want to rehash her lack of a love life. If they talked for a thousand hours, Linda would never understand that life without a husband could be fulfilling, satisfying, rich, varied—all the things her sister associated only with marriage.

"I've been wondering about you and Aaron," Linda said.

The phone rang and Linda jumped to answer it; Dawn was glad for the interruption.

"Darling, I'm so glad you called."

Dawn tactfully went into the den and turned on the TV to give Linda privacy. She hadn't thought about it before, but Linda really did need a phone upstairs in her bedroom. The only one in the house was in the kitchen. They probably planned to hook one up upstairs but hadn't had time to do it yet.

"You can come back," Linda called, her voice exuberant after nearly twenty minutes on the phone with her husband.

"Was he excited about the baby?" Dawn asked, meeting her sister in the dining room.

"Oh, well..."

"You did tell him, didn't you?"

"Not exactly. Well, actually..."

"You didn't!"

"I couldn't just blurt it out on the phone when he's millions of miles away!"

"I understand. Having a baby is so special, you need just the right circumstances to break the news. You did tell him about Aaron being here though, didn't you?"

Linda looked so uncomfortable, Dawn had her answer.

"My ears are burning," Aaron said, stepping into the room through the curtained entrance to the stairs. "Sorry. I didn't mean to eavesdrop. I'm trying to see if I overlooked anything in the storage room, but it's an oven in there today."

"It's okay," Linda said. "You know, I haven't given Lucky any fresh water yet today. Cats are so much easier to take care of. I'll be glad when Gary gets back to do dog duty."

She went out through the mudroom without giving Dawn a chance to go with her.

"I didn't know Linda was expecting." He was frowning in puzzlement.

"She's not very far along. Her husband doesn't even know yet."

"So there's no reason why she should have told me."

"She really feels she should tell him first—actually, second. Linda and I have always told each other everything."

He was wearing cutoffs and a black T-shirt that clung damply to his chest. A fine sprinkling of dark hairs showed above the stretched-out neck band. Dawn wondered how he'd look in a dress shirt and evening wear, but he was too handsome for her peace of mind just as he was.

"Now that you know, you'll understand why you should stop investigating. Linda shouldn't be upset in her condition."

"I don't agree with you."

"Don't you think it's a bad idea to scare a pregnant woman with ghost stories?" She knew she wasn't being entirely fair, but he should have enough sense not to buy into Linda's fantasies at a time like this.

"I think it makes it even more important that I stay and bring this to an acceptable conclusion."

"No, you'll only—"

"Let me ask you, would you say Linda is a highly emotional person?"

"Not the way you mean, no. She has common sense—she's not an airhead."

"I'm not suggesting she is. Pregnancy affects body chemistry. It's not my specialty, by any means, but it's something to consider. If I can put her mind at ease once and for all about what's happening here, it should help insure a safe, happy pregnancy."

"I don't agree ..."

They both heard the door of the mudroom close.

"Linda is going out tonight. We can discuss this then," she said grimly.

Linda came back, and Dawn insisted that she take a turn at fixing lunch.

"You shouldn't skip two meals in a row," she said to him.

"All I need now is some ice water," he said. "I'll help myself."

"I'll fix something for the two of us. You just relax, Dawn," her sister said.

Dawn felt mildly rebuffed and wandered out to the front porch. *Maybe Linda just wanted to be alone with Aaron,* a little voice inside her head suggested. She felt odd man out, not able to share in their belief in the possibility of paranormal experiences. She rocked on the glider with her novel, pretending the words swimming in front of her eyes made some kind of sense.

"I feel so guilty about leaving when I have company," Linda said after dinner that evening. "You two have to ease my conscience by doing something fun yourselves."

"I have my postcard album to price," Dawn quickly mentioned.

"Maybe I shouldn't go," Linda suggested.

"What is there to do in the area?" Aaron asked.

"There's live entertainment at Barney's Grill on Friday nights—that's tonight," Linda said. "If you like country music, that is. Ottawa doesn't have a movie theater, but there's a bowling alley and a roller rink. Dawn was a good skater! I used to really envy her, the way she could dance and do all the fancy stuff."

"It's been a long time," Dawn said. "I'll just stick with my postcards. You don't need to worry about entertaining me."

"I need to be entertained," Aaron teased. "We should try the roller rink."

"I really don't think so."

"Maybe I'd better stay home," Linda said with a convincing pout.

"Linda, go! You need to meet more people. After all, you can't spend all your time at home."

"Only if I'm sure you two have something to do."

"We'll go skating," Aaron said.

"That's not a good idea."

"You're right. I could break a leg and have to spend the summer cooped up in my condo with a cast from my ankle to my hip. I'd have to give up ghost hunting."

"Maybe we should go." Dawn wasn't serious, but she did remember trailing after him that first day, climbing the ladder, crawling behind the furnace, braving the spider-infested depths of the basement. Maybe she should see how he'd do on her kind of turf.

"It's a date," he said before she could back out.

"No, it's not a date, but I guess it beats doing aerobics in front of the TV with a perfect size four in spandex, which is what I need to do after a few days of Linda's wonderful cooking."

"I like spandex," he said, pretending he wasn't elated at the prospect of skating with Dawn in his arms.

Soon—too soon—she was sitting beside him in the front of his cherry-red Jeep as he tried to follow Linda's directions for getting to the rink.

"I've probably forgotten how to skate. I should have my head examined for agreeing to this," she said.

"Ahem." He cleared his throat for effect. "I could give you an eleven p.m. appointment. To have your head examined, that is."

"Thank you, Doctor, but I'm probably too normal to be interesting." She'd rather bare her soul to Bart Simpson!

The worst of it was, she was excited about the crudely arranged "date." He looked terrific in black jeans that fit perfectly in all the right places, and a red knit shirt, definitely his best color. She was glad she'd borrowed Linda's peach short-shorts and a sleeveless, white eyelet blouse that left a few inches of bare midriff.

Was he attracted to Dawn because he wanted her to be something she wasn't? Aaron wondered, remembering how his ex-wife's skepticism and lack of support had hurt in the early years of their marriage. He wished he could see into her head as easily as he could see the outline of her bra and her creamy skin through the little holes in the blouse. He wondered whether she'd dressed in the alluring outfit to tease him—to get even for maneuvering her into going out with him. He hoped she didn't suspect how much he was enjoying her lean, shapely legs in the skimpy shorts.

The parking lot wasn't just crowded, it was jam-packed. They had to leave his Jeep along the side of the road and walk back to the rink.

"This must be the place to go on Friday nights," he said, pleased that she let him hold her arm as they walked.

They walked through the entrance and stopped at a table where a pair of teenagers were manning the cash box and stamping hands.

"How much for two?" he asked one of the girls, holding out a twenty. "We'll need to rent skates."

Dawn held out her hand and a pretty girl with frizzy red hair pounded a rubber stamp against an ink pad and branded her with a smiley face logo.

"You can skip me," Aaron said.

"I'm supposed to stamp everyone," the girl insisted, crinkling her tiny nose in disapproval.

"Toothpaste will take it off," Dawn said.

He held out his hand, wondering if he was going to make a fool of himself, then followed Dawn into the rink.

She said something to him, but he missed it over the blare of music blasting out of overhead speakers.

"What did you say?"

"How long has it been since you skated?" she shouted.

"A couple of years, maybe," he said, telling a whopper of a half-truth.

They weren't the oldest ones there. He saw a gray-haired couple whip by, followed by a gang of pint-size girls giggling and squealing at each other.

He didn't know the procedure, but he followed Dawn, playing the gentleman by getting down on one knee and lacing her skates.

"A little tighter please," she said.

She moved around, testing the skates and getting her balance, while he put on a pair of battered black ones with fluorescent green laces. He stood gingerly, testing for pain points, trying not to think of how his feet felt crammed into the leather-and-steel instruments of torture.

Roller skating was nothing but rolling forward on little wheels; he could do it. He carefully inched up to the waist-high wooden boards that separated the spectators from the skaters, gratefully hanging on to it for a minute.

"There's an opening. Now," she said, taking his hand and propelling them both into the fast-moving stream of bodies.

Blades and ice he could handle; what could be so hard about wheels and wood?

He was on his feet and moving, and it didn't take a genius to figure out where to put his arm. The music was so loud he could imagine coasting on sound waves alone, but at least it was a relatively civilized waltz. He could match the rhythm.

Her waist was small and firm, and he liked the gentle swell of her hip under his fingers. She laughed at a wild-haired adolescent who whistled at her as he breezed past them, then pointed out a little whiz on skates who was scarcely out of diapers.

The music stopped and they rolled up to the boards, laughing and trying to catch their breaths. They'd been around six times, and he'd rediscovered his calf muscles.

"Ladies' choice," a gravelly voice boomed over the loudspeaker. "Come on, girls. Look 'em over good. Here's your chance."

"Tough decision," she said.

"Would you like a soda or something?" he asked.

"What, and miss my chance to do the picking?" She eyed the crowd. "Darn, that blonde got to him first! Well, you'll have to do, I guess."

"You're really inflating my ego," he said, but he loved her teasing.

"Come on." His arm felt wonderful on her back.

This round wasn't for amateurs, he quickly learned. The music was so loud and fast he didn't have time to analyze what kind it was, and all the show-offs came out of the woodwork.

"You're sure you've done this before?" she shouted over the din, amazed that his cologne packed such a punch in the midst of so many overheated bodies.

He nodded miserably, still trying to zero in on the difference between ice and roller skating. For one thing, his hockey skates had never compressed his toes into two numb lumps.

She speeded up, trailed her fingers down to the tips of his, then broke away, rushing ahead in a solo dance so graceful he was afraid his tongue would hit the floor. She looked as though she'd been born on skates, but nothing about her reminded him of a Roller Derby queen. She wasn't muscular or powerful, but she moved like a ballerina on skates: sure, graceful, and beautiful. He wanted to catch up and hold her in his arms again.

The floor tilted, and for an instant he was out of control, not knowing which way he'd be thrown. He grabbed at air, over-corrected, then plopped down in a humiliating pratfall.

Skates roared past him, vicious engines of destruction, and he could imagine his fingers smashed like shelled nuts under a steamroller.

She came back around to him at breakneck speed and offered her hand. He shrugged it off and dragged himself onto his knees, feeling like someone had swatted his rear with a two-by-four.

"Are you okay?" The concerned look in her eyes was nearly worth the embarrassment. Aaron simply nodded.

"You said you could skate." She looked on in concern as he managed to limp to safety.

"I grew up in Milwaukee." He wanted to rub his seat, but it didn't seem manly. "We skated on ice, not greased tilt-a-wheels."

She laughed, a light, happy sound that made him willing to forgive any ridicule she might heap on him.

"Poor Aaron. You're all dusty." She was so relieved he wasn't seriously hurt, she patted his sore bottom. "Let me buy you a soda."

They watched from the sidelines, then tried again. She'd said something about getting back on the horse, but it wasn't the challenge of mastering the skates that sent him out into the bedlam of the rink again. He wanted to put his arms around her, and it didn't bother him at all that she thought she was holding him up.

He couldn't believe it when the voice on the loudspeaker announced the last number. "Grab your sweetie, and do it right."

They were playing something he almost recognized, and it didn't matter if he had to spend the rest of the summer nursing his aches and pains. He was having fun, the real kind that had to do with laughing and playing—and loving.

When the music stopped, dull yellow lights revealed a barnlike room with noisy people crowding the benches to take off their skates. The magic went away when the colored spotlights were extinguished, but Dawn wished it could go on all night. She put her arm around Aaron's waist and hugged him against the side of her hip, wondering how much of this she'd regret in the morning.

"I can't believe you were never on roller skates before," she said, hardly able to restrain herself from touching his raven black hair as he knelt to unlace her skates.

"The kids in my neighborhood played hockey—ice hockey in winter, street hockey in the summer. My younger brother was good, but I was a better swimmer than a skater."

"Do you still swim?" She could easily imagine him streaking through the water, fit and trim as an Olympic hopeful.

"When I can."

"Did you have other brothers or sisters?" She was suddenly struck by how little she knew about him as a person. It wasn't because she never thought about him.

"No, just my brother, Nathan. My father was a high school phys ed teacher and swim coach. My mother taught English. We were a pretty ordinary family, I guess."

"Sounds nice to me." She wondered whether his father had a beard and dark, kind eyes like his older son.

"Are you as hungry as I am?" He took her hand in his as they went to drop off the skates.

"Hungry enough to try Barney's Grill."

When they got to the roadside entertainment spot, a waitress in white boots and a black leather skirt as skimpy as Dawn's shorts studied the crowded room and pointed out a pair of stools at a high table in a dark corner. Those close to the small stage sat at heavy, varnished picnic tables, but the patrons in the rear all sat on elevated perches.

The seat felt sticky on her bare thighs, so Dawn sat close to the edge, hooking her white-sneakered feet onto the iron stool supports. She noticed that Aaron sat down gingerly, but her smile wasn't mocking. She admired him for plunging into the swirling mass of skaters and giving it his best try.

"The Barney burger and fries is probably the safest bet," he said.

"That's what I'm having." His smile was so warm, she wanted to trace the outline of his lips with her little finger.

They drank a pitcher of dark draft beer, dipped their fries into ketchup, and polished off the contents of two paper-lined plastic baskets down to the last dill pickle.

"More fun than Monopoly?" he kidded, not able to remember the last time being with a woman had been such a delight.

"Much more fun than Trivial Pursuit sports questions. I hate losing!"

"So do I, if it's my fault. But I don't beat myself up over games of chance. I had fun tonight." That was like saying the ocean was a little damp.

"I did, too." She wiped her lips, wondering if they would feel slippery when Aaron kissed her. If he wanted to kiss her. Why was she so sure they would come to that?

She reminded herself of a whole list of sobering reasons for backing away from him, but she did love the way his brows moved when his face registered emotion. Taken feature by feature, his face wasn't exceptionally handsome—well, not extraordinary, anyway—but she could read so many good things in the pleasing planes and angles and in his smoldering dark eyes: compassion, humor, dignity, strength—and passion.

After they finished eating, she hated to have the evening end. On the stage a three-piece band was performing, long-haired young men in tattered jeans and plaid shirts too ragged to donate to the Salvation Army and a red-bearded singer who played a guitar and wailed about his lover's betrayal. His song was romantic even if it wasn't very melodic, and she was swept into the pathos of his emotions. She wanted to hug him and tell him things would be all right. When he finished and the performers left the stage for a break, she clapped as loudly as anyone in the room.

"You enjoy country music," he said, a statement, not a question.

"I've never thought about it very much one way or the other, but he's good, don't you think?"

"I think you're good."

"Me, good?" She laughed. "In grading antiques, good means not so good—battered, beat up, showing age."

"That's not the kind of good I meant. Try imaginative, lively, thoughtful..."

"I didn't mean to fish for compliments."

"You don't need to. It's a pleasure being here with you, Dawn. Most of the really nice women in the world seem to be taken."

"Uh-oh. Are you going to ask me why a nice girl like me isn't married?"

She took a sip of beer and wiped the foam from her upper lip with the tip of her tongue; it was a job he would have liked to do for her.

"No, not unless you want to tell a friend."

She hadn't thought of him as a friend, only as an adversary, a man who attracted her against her better judgment. But somehow she knew he'd be a wonderful friend: warm, considerate, witty.

"I came so close once I could smell the orange blossoms," she said, "but maybe I was lucky. I take 'till death do us part' pretty seriously, and he didn't even stick around until the ink on the invitations was dry."

"I'm sorry. I've been there, and I know it hurts. My ex-wife had the perfect life planned. A house in the suburbs, a luxury car and a van in the garage, two perfectly behaved kids. It was a color-by-number scenario, but I was about as important as the potted plant on the front porch. My doctoral degree made good window dressing, but she wanted me to have an upscale practice."

"I've heard that divorce can be a harder separation than death. It robs you of all the good memories."

Her eyes were soft and dreamy, more green than hazel in the recessed light, and he didn't doubt her sincerity. She had depths he was only beginning to glimpse, compassion and understanding that she kept hidden from casual acquaintances.

He smiled at her with so much admiration she could feel a tingle all the way to toes numb from clinging to the high stool. She felt warmed, not threatened, by his intense gaze, and for a few moments it was enough to just look at each other.

"Linda will wonder where we are," she said, not really wanting to go.

"Don't worry about Linda."

"I do, though."

"She's not as fragile as you think. She doesn't need mothering."

"If I'm too protective, it's because I don't know what to make of her hearing things no one else hears. That worries me a lot."

He wanted to reassure her about his motives, to convince her he was driven by curiosity, a desire to solve the riddles of the unknown, and concern for people like Linda who were terrorized by it, but he sensed she wasn't ready to believe him.

"Linda told me about your family, your father deserting you, and your mother having to manage alone."

"We had some bad times, but we got through them together." Part of her longed to trust him, but she couldn't reconcile this gentle, understanding man with the ghost hunter who chased spooky things.

"I guess it's time to go." She reluctantly started to slide off the stool, but he took her hand, willing her not to run away from him.

"I've been thinking about you a lot."

He squeezed her hand enough to make her feel cherished, and she had to force herself to remember who he was and why he was in her life.

Her feet touched the floor, and he released her. She was right. It was time to go. He was tempted to say things she wasn't ready to hear—and he had to sort out his own feelings before he made another serious mistake. He was only beginning to realize how much he cared for Dawn. Unfortunately she seemed to post a No Trespassing sign on her emotional life, but he felt sure there was a warm, passionate woman under her guarded exterior. She was as skeptical about the paranormal as his ex-wife had been, but there was nothing cold or unemotional in her makeup. Still, he didn't know if they could get beyond this hurdle.

When they got to the parking lot, he opened the door for her, deciding to follow her lead for the rest of the evening. If she didn't want to talk...

"Do you remember the way back to Linda's?" She sounded concerned, so he took her seriously.

"I think County Road HH will take us over to—"

"Do you know where HH is?"

"We turn right going out of the parking lot, then left at the first stop sign."

"I'm glad you have a sense of direction. I don't have the foggiest idea how to get back from here."

"I'll try not to get lost," he promised.

A bright yellow light glowed over the front porch door, and a small table lamp lit their way into the living room.

"Linda must be home. Those are her keys in the candy dish."

Dawn moved quietly into the dining room and eased open the door to the spare room. Her sister was asleep on the air mattress, a sheet tangled around her bare legs. Dawn resisted an urge to straighten her cover, wondering if she should try to be less protective of her sister.

"She's asleep," she told Aaron when she returned to the dining room.

"Good." He came close, speaking in a husky whisper.

"Thank you. I had a nice time." Her mother had taught her to say this before her first date in the ninth grade. She'd never said it so stiffly... or meant it so passionately. She wouldn't forget tonight.

"It was my pleasure." He'd made a fool of himself at the rink, but he wouldn't forget the impact Dawn had had on him when she skated. He hadn't had so much fun in a long time, and he didn't want it to end.

"Are you...?" She started to ask if he planned to sleep in Linda's bed, but the question suddenly seemed too personal.

"Am I what?"

"Keeping watch," she said, trying to sound disinterested.

"I want to hear what Linda heard. If it doesn't happen..."

"You'll admit it's all in her head?"

"Not necessarily." He was tired of this argument, tired of the paranormal intruding on the here and now, tired of not kissing her the way he needed to kiss her.

"Dawn." He spoke her name in a sensual whisper.

"I'm... I'm tired."

"Me, too." He stepped closer, reaching out to touch a strand of hair brushing against her cheek. Her features were indistinct in the dim light, but he saw her lips part and her eyelids flicker shut.

She said good-night, but her words were meaningless. Beckoning him closer with emotional magnetism, she was as still as a statue waiting to be blessed with the gift of life.

He was going to kiss her—had planned to since she'd set him on fire by patting the seat of his jeans. But what he felt wasn't sex—wasn't just sex. His legs trembled, but he didn't blame it on overexertion.

She came into his arms, reaching up to bury her fingers in his hair, sending shock waves down his spine. He didn't even recognize the beast within that wanted to ravish her mouth and tear the scraps of cloth away from her body.

Taking a deep breath like a man about to take a plunge on a roller coaster, he wrapped his arms around her, banishing the beast and kissing her with slow, soul-searing intensity.

It felt like her first kiss ever. Her lips throbbed, and she pressed them against the sharp ivory ridges of his teeth. All her senses absorbed his sweet masculinity, and she shivered with pleasure when he moved his hand under her blouse, kneading the taut flesh and manipulating the stubborn hooks until her bra snapped loose.

"This blouse," he whispered, "has been driving me crazy."

"It's Linda's." She was assigning blame to her sister, but she knew the truth: for the first time since adolescence, she'd dressed to look deliberately sexy. Later she would feel guilty and question her motives, the kind of soul-searching she practiced so ruthlessly. Now all she felt was a vibrant excitement. She belonged in Aaron's arms.

His hand moved to her breast, gently cupping it, slowly moving the tips of his fingers like a blind man learning to define the world by shape and texture.

The moan began deep in her being, a honeyed cry of ecstasy. He lowered his head, running his lips over the velvety softness of her throat, deciding whether to carry or lead her to a surface more hospitable than the hard oak planks of the dining room table.

"Dawn, is that you?"

He didn't need the panicky shove she gave him. In some obscure way, he was violating Linda's trust. He didn't want her to see him like this: aroused, inebriated by passion, naked in his need.

Dawn gestured frantically toward the stairs; he was annoyed by her urgency but grateful for the curtain that parted silently, letting him duck into the stairwell. He crept halfway up before he realized the steps were as noisy and discordant as an orchestra warming up for a concert. He walked the rest of the way, mad at himself for acting like a schoolboy up to no good.

Linda was sitting up on the air mattress and looking for her fuzzy pink slippers when Dawn opened the door.

"Sorry we woke you." She said "we" without thinking, but, of course, Linda had manipulated them into going out together.

"Did you have fun?" Linda sounded wide awake; Dawn wondered if she'd been listening for them.

"Sort of. Aaron fell at the rink. He didn't give himself time to get the hang of it before he tried to race."

"Just like a man." Linda's tone was amused and indulgent. "He didn't hurt himself, did he?"

"Only his pride. Well, he may have to sleep on his stomach." She felt hot, prickly, flustered. The last thing she wanted was a session of girl talk with her sister. "Go back to sleep. I'll talk to you in the morning."

"Dawn, I'm scared."

"Oh, honey, don't be!" She knelt on the mattress, her knees pushing aside the air to rest against hard floor. "Do you want me to stay here with you?"

"No, of course not." Linda's amusement was genuine. "I'd feel silly. I'm not afraid down here, just worried because I don't know what happened to me."

A demonic shape suddenly streaked by Dawn and she cried out in fright, her soft shriek quickly turning to laughter.

"I didn't know you were sleeping with Simba."

"She's not the best roommate."

"I take it we were disturbing her." Dawn needed to laugh; the cat was a good excuse.

"Don't worry. She comes and goes as she likes, except when Gary's home to lock her in the mudroom at night. Just leave the door open a crack so she can come back if she wants to."

"You're sure you want to stay down here by yourself?"

"Sure. I'll be asleep before you get to the top of the stairs."

Aaron had left the hall light on for her. She climbed the stairs slowly, wondering what she wanted to happen when she reached the top. Her short exchange with Linda had served as a badly needed cold shower. She'd never felt quite the way she had tonight.

Aaron was stretched out on the bed, wondering if the moment had been destroyed, the magic exposed as an illusion. His heartbeat was rapid, his groin ached, and he didn't even want to inventory his other pains. He'd slipped out of his shoes and jeans but was otherwise dressed.

This investigation wasn't like any other he'd ever done. He felt he had a personal stake in the outcome, something that went beyond adding to his store of knowledge and satisfying his need to reach out to troubled people. What part did Dawn play in this sense of urgency? Was he imagining the way she affected him, seducing himself into feeling need again after the long period of emptiness in his life?

He agonized over whether to back off or listen to his heart, then he heard Dawn on the stairs and realized she would make the decision for him. Would she seek him out or retreat to her own room? Listening with his breath trapped in his lungs, he heard her stop in front of Linda's bedroom door, the telltale floorboard betraying her as surely as a sophisticated alarm system.

She paused for only an instant, then he knew she was moving down the hallway, toward her room—or his.

Did she stop? Silence mocked him, but her step was too light to draw noisy protests from every board under the carpet.

He knew what he wanted: to hold her in his arms, to feel her flesh against his, to touch— But what he wanted might destroy the fragile beginning they'd made, if that was what it was. Dawn didn't trust him. He read hesitation in her eyes even when she seemed to be most open. Instead of hoping she would take the final step to his room, he worried whether she would make the right decision: the one that would allow them to keep forging new links.

He heard a small squeak; Gary Hall needed to attack the hinges in the house with an oil can.

It was her door, not his. He wouldn't sleep well tonight, but he took hope in the long pause before she made her decision.

Chapter Six

Dawn wanted to be with Aaron. She could hear the sound of her own breathing in the big, lonely room, and she didn't want to spend the night apart from him. If she watched with him again, it would only be a pretext to stay close to him. She hadn't ruled out all her suspicions, but tonight had changed one thing: an invisible wall couldn't protect her from her own feelings.

Lying awake in bed, she was disturbed by the intensity of her longing. She'd come so close to taking those few extra steps to his room.

Was he sleeping? Would he welcome her if she came now? She wanted to feel safe in the circle of his arms, but going to him would be like stepping into another dimension, suspending all her disbelief and accepting him for what he was.

Her legs felt like lead weights, and she didn't have the resolve to make them move. She tried to focus on something soothing, but she kept coming back to Aaron. She didn't believe that what he was doing was good for Linda, but his kisses made her light-headed. When her name rolled off his tongue like buttery icing from a frosting press, she wanted to purr and rub against him like a more affectionate version of Simba.

Was this infatuation? Maybe she had been too long without male company. All she knew for sure was that she wanted to be with him, but the paranormal stood between them.

Aaron burrowed his face into the pillow, unable to put Dawn out of his mind. Instead of counting sheep, he was following her around the rink, watching her circle with skates resounding on the waxy boards. He couldn't keep up with her, not even in his imagination, but he was mesmerized by her energy and grace.

A chilling shriek shattered his daydreams, and he rushed into the hall, not so drowsy he didn't wonder how Linda's voice could sound so loud coming from downstairs. He nearly collided with Dawn, taking her in his arms before he realized she was the one who was screaming.

She broke away and ran down the stairs, and for an instant all he could hear was Lucky's howling and the pounding of blood in his ears.

"Dawn!"

He raced after her, caught her in his arms at the bottom of the steps, and held her close, shocked by her trembling.

"Honey, what is it? You're okay. I'm here."

His voice was low and comforting, and after a few moments she responded to it, relaxing against him with a muffled sob.

"What happened?" Linda came out of her temporary bedroom, snapping her robe as she walked, making Aaron more conscious of Dawn's bare shoulders and thin cotton gown.

She couldn't let Linda see how frightened she was. Reluctantly stepping away from Aaron's arms, she struggled to pull herself together, succeeding for her sister's sake.

"Nothing important," she said, her voice hoarse and crackly. "I heard—"

She froze, suddenly aware of how skimpy her nightgown was and how foolish she must look.

"I think there's a mouse in my room," she said, saying the first thing that came to mind.

"Come into the kitchen," Aaron said, taking her arm and giving her little choice.

What had happened? Her legs were still trembling, and she wasn't even sure whether she'd been sound asleep or still lingering in that hazy state between wakefulness and slumber.

Aaron got her a glass of water and sat down beside her at the table while she drank, giving her time to think of what she should say to Linda.

"I can't believe you saw a mouse," her sister said. "Not with Simba in the house."

"Maybe I was dreaming." It was the only excuse that came to mind.

"You heard something, didn't you?" Linda was wide awake and seemed determined to get a straight story from Dawn.

"Possibly, but it's nothing like you think. I must have..." She thought frantically, desperate not to alarm her sister any more than she already had. "Had a leg cramp. Because I haven't skated in ages. You know how they hurt."

"Are you sure? Does your leg still ache?" Linda was the calm, practical sister now.

"No, my leg is fine. Linda, I have a great idea," she said, trying to sound perky and inspired. "Why don't you come home with me for a visit? You can look up all your old friends and tell them about the baby. I'm still on vacation, so—"

"Dawn, stop it!" her sister interrupted. "I'm not going home with you. Something happened to you, and I have a right to know what."

"I had a dream."

"What kind of dream?" Aaron asked, gently probing.

"Something about a nursery—probably in the room where I was sleeping. There were toys—a rocking horse. I can't remember much."

"You heard it rocking!" Linda said, excitedly.

"No, I don't think what I heard was the horse. You know how dreams vanish when you wake up."

Dawn pursed her lips, pretending to concentrate, but she didn't need to fish around in her memory for details of the dream. She would never forget the peculiar noise or the terrible fluorescent glow that hovered near the foot of the bed, turning her blood to ice.

"I'll go up and look around," Aaron said, anxious to discover the source of the fear he saw in Dawn's eyes.

Dawn watched him leave the room, her heart in her throat and her mind still reeling. She'd rushed into his arms as though her life depended on him, but how could she trust the man who'd just gone upstairs to hunt for evidence of ghosts? She had to get away from this crazy house, from Aaron, and from the way she was beginning to feel about him.

Upstairs Aaron puzzled over the new development, angry at himself because he'd dozed off and couldn't verify what had disturbed Dawn. He'd tried putting his equipment in different locations; it was now in the hall between the master bedroom and the storage room, too far away to have picked up anything in the room where Dawn had been sleeping.

Had that room once been a nursery? He needed to use the resources in the public library and learn more about the house and the families who'd lived there. Thank heavens tomorrow was one of the days the small-town facility was open.

He sat on the edge of the bed where Dawn had been sleeping, tying to keep his mind on the problem at hand. The room was sparsely furnished, and he didn't think there was a physical explanation within the four walls. Was Dawn's experience just a different aspect of Linda's?

Something warm and furry brushed against his bare calf, startling him and breaking his concentration.

"Simba, are you trying to tell me something?" He reached down and stroked her head, rewarded by a deep purring. "Have I been ignoring you? I wonder..."

Minutes later, Aaron, hastily clad in his black jeans, joined the sisters in the kitchen.

"I don't know if we have another player in the game or not," he said, sitting with the big cat on his lap. "Was she in your room when you went to sleep, Dawn?"

"You rascal," Linda said, reaching over to rumple her fur. "I wouldn't put it past her to bed down on Dawn's pillow."

"I didn't see her," Dawn said, then realized Simba was an explanation both she and Linda could accept. "Of course, I didn't look under the bed before I went to sleep."

She looked at Aaron for confirmation, but his face was impassive. He wasn't going to agree to such a simple explanation, at least not until he woke up with those glittering yellow eyes two inches from his face.

Dawn bit her lip, trying to reconcile the cat with the eerie, rhythmic noise that had roused her. Her memory was growing hazy, and it was hard to remember why she'd been so terrified.

"I guess you've done what you came for," she said to Aaron. "You've caught Linda's ghost red-handed."

"I don't think Simba had anything to do with what I heard," Linda pointed out.

Dawn was too embarrassed for further debate. She'd run screaming from her room in her nightgown, alarmed her sister, and given Aaron an opportunity to play hero. She wanted to hide her head under the covers and forget the whole thing.

"Let's get some sleep," Aaron suggested. "It's nearly three a.m."

Linda invited Dawn to share the air mattress downstairs, but she declined. Much to her discomfort, Aaron waited for her to go upstairs. They didn't say anything until they were standing outside her bedroom.

"Thank you for telling Linda such a convincing story," she said. "It could have been the cat all along."

He didn't want lies to stand between them. "You don't believe that any more than I do," he said. "If you're afraid to be in there alone..."

She was—just a little, but she was more afraid of spending the rest of the night with Aaron. More than ever, she didn't understand why he was so obsessed with the paranormal. If what she'd just experienced was a psychic phenomenon—and she denied it vehemently to herself—she never wanted to have anything to do with another one. Were other people's fears exciting to him? She shivered, said good-night, and hurried into the bedroom, closing the door behind her.

Aaron turned out the light in his room, not expecting more occurrences that night, but he stood by the window for a long time, not really seeing anything in the darkness beyond the pane of glass. Blaming the cat had only muddied the water more between Dawn and him. Worse, he realized he'd bought into Dawn's skeptical belief that Linda was imagining things. Now he was almost sure this wasn't the case.

Linda had taken him into her home on faith, and so far he'd let her down. Dawn had distracted him, and somewhere along the line he must have missed something.

If anything serious happened, he would have to blame his own carelessness. He had to put Dawn out of his mind—beginning now so he could get some sleep during what was left of the night.

Amazingly, she slept, not waking until the room was bright and sunny. Her bad experience was only an embarrassing memory, and she tested her nerve by opening the closet door at the end of the room. Except for a faint odor of moth crystals, it was entirely benign. Still, she didn't feel like lingering in the room—or anywhere else upstairs.

Telling herself she wanted to try the big, claw-footed tub, she carried her clothes and travel kit downstairs, not looking for Aaron on the way. Memories of their fun at the skating rink were overshadowed by her nightmare. Maybe when she went home, she would regret not getting closer to him, but it was a risk she had to take. She saw the way he reacted to her fear: compassionate but avidly curious, too. Maybe he wasn't a fraud, but it was even more unsettling to think he wanted to find evidence to prove there were horrible things like ghosts—tortured souls of the dead wandering around scaring people. She'd always thought of hauntings in connection with Halloween or spooky movies, and she wanted to keep it that way.

Aaron had already left the house when Dawn met her sister in the kitchen for breakfast.

"You know what Aaron did, don't you?" Linda asked, looking ill at ease.

"What?"

"His story about the cat. He didn't want you to be upset."

"Me? He did that for you!" She couldn't believe what Linda was suggesting.

"No. Aaron knows I'm still scared."

"Then why won't you come home with me?"

"That isn't a solution. Gary and I own this house. We want it to be our home until we're ready for the old folks' home. We've done so much—stripped woodwork, painted, varnished, papered—everything we have is invested here. I think Aaron can help us if I give him enough time."

"What can he possibly do?" Dawn hated this conversation.

"He can find out whether we have a good ghost or a bad one."

"You don't have any ghost!"

"Well, if we do, I sure hope it's a friendly one. One thing is certain—I'm burning with curiosity about what he can discover. Some people treat their ghost like a member of the family. It's like having an eccentric relative drop in once in a while."

"I don't believe you."

"Really," Linda cheerfully assured her. "People sometimes live with a ghost for years and are happy to have it. The important thing is not to be afraid."

"Aren't you afraid?"

"I certainly was at first, but now I don't know. Maybe our ghost is bad, maybe not."

"I don't know what to say." Dawn remembered her own terror only too well, but she couldn't—wouldn't—admit it had anything to do with dead spirits floating around. Somehow she'd slipped into the Twilight Zone. That couldn't be her real sister, blithely talking about good and bad ghosts.

* * *

The Ottawa library was almost as old as the town itself and was housed in a small, stone building grayed by age. Two girls on bikes and an elderly lady with a straw hat were waiting for the door to open when Aaron got there, and he had to wait until the librarian changed the sign to Open before he could ask for help.

"I know the old Hoover place," she said, using a key to unlock the local history room. "That young couple has done a fine job fixing it up. The Hoovers were a prominent family, so you'll find some good references here. You can work in here. We only keep it locked to discourage children from handling fragile materials."

Aaron knew from past experience the kind of information he needed.

"I'll be fine on my own," he assured the petite, white-haired librarian. He would have meant it before he met Dawn. Now he wasn't sure of anything except that he wanted to resolve this case.

Dawn knew Aaron wasn't accountable to her, but she was vaguely worried when he didn't return to the house for lunch or dinner.

"He said not to expect him until after the library closes at eight," Linda said.

They played a desultory game of gin rummy until Linda won so many times she quit.

"You're not paying attention," she complained. "You threw me three queens in a row."

"Sorry, I'm not much of a player anymore."

"You have your mind on Aaron, don't you?"

"I'd like to know what he's up to."

"That's not what I meant. You haven't said much about your date."

"We had fun. I told you that."

"I want to know if it was 'special' fun."

"I suppose it could have been . . . but we're too different. I'm never sure what he's thinking."

"A little mystery in a man is exciting."

"This paranormal stuff isn't. I hate it!"

"Why? Because you're afraid? Or do you think you're too smart to buy into things you can't see?"

Linda rarely spoke so bluntly, and Dawn was surprised into telling what she really thought.

"People have been chasing ghosts for centuries. No one has ever caught up with one, as far as I know. I just prefer to focus on real things . . . things I can see, hear, touch."

"No one knew what an atom was a century ago. I've never seen one, but I believe they must exist. Maybe, with all the right equipment—"

"I can't believe we're having this discussion. Please, Linda, don't try to convert me. You'll be happier, too, when you forget about it."

"When I can forget about it," her sister corrected her, jumping up when a Jeep drove into the driveway.

Aaron walked into the porch, and Dawn froze, not wanting to seem as eager to see him as she was.

"I think," he said without preliminaries, "it's time for the three of us to talk."

Chapter Seven

They chose the kitchen without discussing it, gravitating toward it because it was a warm, friendly place.

"I want you to know everything I know," he said solemnly, "but you don't have to accept my conclusions.... There are no quick, easy explanations for paranormal occurrences. Even when everything points to one solution, there's always controversy. It's hard to get two investigators to agree on a probable cause, let alone convince skeptics."

Dawn watched him with reservation, not as keen as Linda to hear his theories. Everything he said seemed to put them further apart.

"You both heard a noise, either in your heads or actually in the house," Aaron said, tensed to get through what he'd decided to tell them.

Dawn watched his eyes, thinking how dark and complex they were—and how they'd softened with passion when he'd taken her in his arms. It was the wrong time for thoughts like that, but part of her didn't want him to say anything to destroy what they'd so briefly shared.

"I wasn't able to record the sound, even though I had equipment set up in the storage room or the hallway every night. But what I think you both heard was the rocking of a chair."

"A rocking horse would sound something like that." Dawn remembered her dream and saw the logic in his thinking, but she didn't understand how it could be true.

"It wasn't necessarily a real sound, but it seems to have been something like the sound a mother would make rocking her child," he said.

"Like Louisa Hoover might have made rocking one of her babies," Linda said.

"You expect us to believe in a real ghost?" Dawn was shocked. Deep inside, she'd nurtured hope that Aaron really could clear up the mystery.

"Remember, I'm only talking theories. Someday science will get a handle on the paranormal experiences people attribute to ghosts. They could be related to psychic experiences."

"Like people who can detect murderers by touching one of their victims?" Linda asked.

"I don't buy that!" Dawn was anxiously watching her sister, convinced Aaron was doing more harm than good.

"That's theory, too, not fact," he was quick to remind them. "Dawn and I talked about objects acting as recording devices, playing back emotional traumas."

"Like an old radio," Dawn said, wanting his lecture to end. She didn't know nearly enough about this man, but she had hoped for more from him.

"I could never be afraid of a mother rocking her baby," Linda said thoughtfully. "Even a ghostly mother."

"I think I may be able to bring my investigation to a conclusion if both of you are willing. But we won't try this unless you believe me on one thing. In all the countless thousands of sightings in recorded history, there has never, ever been a documented case of a paranormal phenomenon physically harming a living being."

After he talked to them about his plan, Dawn escaped to the front porch, desperately needing time to think about what he'd said. The evening was cool, and she pressed her cheek against the armrest of the glider, hoping the cold metal would make her feel less feverish. Her mind was a muddle, and she felt betrayed. Aaron hadn't promised her anything; he hadn't broken his word, but she felt let down, totally deflated. She couldn't begin to guess what the outcome of his plan would be, but it was too late to stop herself from loving him.

She watched the sky darken, but not even the one perfect moment when the sky was a deep midnight blue before turning black was enough to lift her spirits. She didn't watch for the first star of evening. There was nothing to wish for, except possibly that Linda wouldn't be hurt by his plan.

"Are you asleep?" Aaron's voice was a husky whisper.

She was tempted to pretend she was, but he didn't give her a chance. He sat down beside her, making the glider chains squeak.

"Are you cold?" He put his arm around her shoulders.

"No." She stiffened, not trusting herself so close to him. "Please don't."

He moved his arm away.

"I think knowing more about the manifestation, if there is one, will help put Linda's mind at ease. She's probably been imagining demonic possession, headless specters, ancient Indian graves under the basement, all the stuff in horror books and movies," he explained uneasily. "I think the Hoovers were pretty ordinary people who had a lot of sadness in their lives losing three children."

"Louisa the Friendly Ghost?" She was so upset her voice sounded strangled.

"Is the possibility of a benevolent ghost so terrible? Do you think it would be better to let Linda worry about some malevolent spirit with a bloody ax lurking in the upstairs hall?"

"You want her to believe in fables, legends, silly, incredible stories." She was shivery, hugging herself so he wouldn't notice.

"All I'm trying to do is give her some peace of mind. I could be wrong. We may not see anything tonight."

"If you want to reassure her, why not just tell her there's no such thing as a supernatural happening?"

"She wouldn't believe me."

"You don't know that."

"Be reasonable, Dawn. Linda has a right to know if something paranormal is happening here. The truth is probably less dramatic than a runaway imagination. And less frightening."

"If planting the idea of a chair-rocking ghost is your idea of compassion..."

"There isn't one right way to explain away what both of you experienced," he said, beginning to sound less patient. "Don't try to make me the bad guy."

"I don't know what you are," she said miserably. "Maybe you think you're being kind..."

"This isn't just about Linda, is it?"

"Of course it is."

"Your sister is an adult. She has ideas of her own about what happened to her. At least she's open-minded enough to consider all the possibilities."

"I don't think we have anything else to talk about." She started to leave, but he was too quick, standing and putting his hands on her shoulders, facing her on the dark porch.

"Forget about your sister for a minute. What about us?"

Don't let him kiss me, she thought, willing herself to resist the undeniable chemistry between them.

He groped for the right thing to say. "Let's talk about why this is such a problem between us."

"I don't like what you're doing."

"All I'm trying to do is shed a little light. Whether I'm right or wrong, we'll take it from there. Linda understands that. I can't tell her what's going to happen tonight—maybe nothing—but I'm going to do my best to clear this up."

How could he get through to her? Why did he care so much? He dropped his hands, frustrated by the inadequacy of words but sure he couldn't resolve their differences by taking her in his arms and kissing her, however much he wanted to do just that.

She saw herself through his eyes, and it didn't make her feel good. He must think she was stubborn, opinionated, and unwilling to give up her role as Linda's protector. She was also frightened—but not of ghosts. She cared too much about Aaron, but she was afraid of trusting him; old hurts ran too deep.

"I guess you'll be leaving when this experiment is over," she said.

"We'll see what happens." He turned and left her standing there alone.

One hot, wet tear trickled down Dawn's cheek, and she tried to remember all the reasons why she was right to oppose him.

They met later in the big bedroom Dawn had been using. She'd moved all her things into the spare room downstairs more than an hour earlier.

Now that it was nearly midnight, she couldn't believe that three rational, intelligent adults were sitting in semi-darkness waiting for a ghost.

Aaron had set the stage by carrying the old rocking chair from the storage room into this room, the one the Hoovers had used as a nursery. He'd confirmed it at the library. The house had been designed by a local architect, and the floor plan appeared in a biography written by one of his descendants. Aaron hadn't left any stones unturned in his search for the Hoover family history.

He left the door open a crack, letting a narrow shaft of light fall across the floor midway between the bed where they sat and the empty rocker.

Dawn sat beside Linda on the bed, leaning on pillows propped against the carved headboard. Aaron took a position slightly to the side of the bed, sitting on a metal folding chair.

Linda repeatedly cleared her throat, and Dawn felt as if she were fighting for a breath of air. She didn't expect to see anything, but sitting in a dark room in absolute silence took a toll on her nerves. She certainly didn't want to hear that eerie noise again.

Aaron was sitting by Linda's side of the bed, and Dawn could see well enough to know when he reached out and took her sister's hand. The believers united against one lonely skeptic, she thought miserably, wondering how long they'd have to sit staring at an empty rocker before the ghost hunter admitted defeat.

"What time is it?" Linda whispered after they'd been there for an eternity and then some.

"One-fifty-seven," Aaron said.

"I thought ghosts were supposed to walk at midnight." Dawn was restless, uneasy, upset with herself for agreeing to this charade, but she didn't think any part of her agitation was fear. It seemed too incredible that all three of them would imagine the same thing or have the same dream, so she only wanted it to be over with. She didn't want to remember she and Linda had both experienced something similar separately....

Linda whimpered, a sound Aaron interpreted as the first signal that something was going to happen.

"Don't move or make a sound," he whispered urgently.

A dim light seemed to come from nowhere, throwing the rocking chair into sharper relief.

Dawn felt as if she were watching a high school play with the stage set for the opening scene. She was tense with anticipation but not expecting anything to materialize. Maybe Aaron could use his skills as a psychologist to manipulate minds. He had gotten them to agree to this charade, much against her better judgment.

Then the noise began, rasping and creaking, the familiar rhythmic sound of a wooden rocker moving on the bare boards of a floor.

She heard her sister's sharp intake of breath, and then she was too startled to notice anything but a luminous, liquid shape hovering over the rocker. She was mesmerized for the few short moments it took the figure to assemble itself into a recognizable shape—the image of a mother holding an infant in her arms.

The room went totally black and Dawn frantically blinked her eyes, wondering if she'd been struck blind. This instant passed, too, and she saw the shaft of yellow light again, dimly illuminating an empty, motionless chair.

"Did you see?" Linda asked breathlessly.

"I saw her," Dawn admitted, too stunned to question the evidence of her own eyes.

She wanted to hear what Aaron would say, but he seemed lost in thought. None of them made any move to leave the room.

"I wasn't afraid," Linda said, sounding astonished and awed at the same time.

Aaron felt as if he'd waited half his life for this brief glimpse of something beyond man's known boundaries. He'd experienced cold spots, recorded odd air patterns, even heard sounds that seemed to come from nowhere, but he'd never seen a true manifestation of a human form. He knew how it must have felt to see the first bacteria under a microscope or to focus the first telescope on the night sky.

He hadn't tried to record the sound or focus a video camera on the manifestation. The mystic in him didn't believe a miracle could be captured on tape. Tomorrow he might regret this uncharacteristic laxness, but now it was enough that he had seen.

He was still holding Linda's hand; her right hand was locked in Dawn's. He'd never felt closer to other human beings.

Eventually they said good-night and parted, Dawn joining her sister on the air mattress and Aaron retreating to the front upstairs bedroom where his things were. By tacit agreement, they decided not to talk too much about it until morning. It was the kind of experience that had to be absorbed by a solitary individual before it could be dissected in the light of day.

Dawn didn't think she could sleep, but she blacked out almost instantly.

They met over toast and coffee in the morning, but Dawn had already confirmed that Linda had seen exactly what she had.

"You saw Louisa, too, didn't you?" Linda asked when Aaron came into the kitchen with his hair and beard still curling damply from the shower.

"It could have been a mass hallucination," he suggested gently, not wanting to add to Dawn's haggard look of puzzlement.

"You don't believe that," she said woodenly. "I saw something odd, but I'm not sure I want it explained."

"I'm pretty sure I can't explain it. Were either of you frightened?"

They both confirmed with a head shake that they hadn't been.

"It was beautiful, in a way," Linda said. "Is there anything we can do to help her?"

"Maybe just seeing her, acknowledging her sorrow by being there for her, will be enough comfort to put her soul to rest," he said pensively.

"I felt so sorry for her," Linda said.

"You don't think it will happen again?" Dawn couldn't deny that something had appeared, but she wasn't ready to give that shimmering form a name or assign motive to it.

"Maybe the manifestation was possible only because all three of us were there to provide an energy field," he suggested.

"Do you want to watch again tonight?" Linda asked.

"It's up to you. I want to do whatever will make you feel safe."

"Oddly enough, I feel that way already. If I watched again, it would only be to satisfy my curiosity. Maybe that isn't a good enough reason. Sort of like window-peeping into another world."

Aaron was pleased by her insight; Linda had leapt to the same conclusion that he'd reached after hours of sleepless thought. He'd been given a great gift; maybe it was enough just to cherish it.

He looked at Dawn, wanting to see the same sparkle of excitement and understanding in her eyes, but she just looked stunned, as though her world had just been turned upside down. He could only guess at the complex maze of feelings and beliefs she had to sort out.

"Dawn, how do you feel about it?" he asked gently.

She shook her head. "Don't ask me. I'm really not sure. Linda should decide what to do. After all, it's her ghost."

He didn't correct her. "Paranormal phenomenon" didn't seem an adequate label for what they'd seen.

They were still sipping coffee at the kitchen table, not saying much, when Jane called.

"I hate interrupting your vacation," Dawn's partner said. "I've known about this since the day you left, but I tried to convince myself I don't need you. I do!"

"What's wrong?"

"The worst! Derek and I are being audited by the IRS. You keep all the financial records for the mall, and I'm going to sound like an absolute idiot when they ask me questions."

"I'm sure everything will be fine. Maybe they're mostly interested in Derek's income."

"No. I think the mall is their target. Frankly, I'm scared."

"When is the audit?"

"I should have told you sooner! It's Tuesday. Can you possibly go with us? My husband thinks I'm worrying for nothing, but you know Derek. He could stay calm in a tornado."

"I want to go. It's my responsibility." She immediately thought of her sister. Now she had the perfect reason for insisting Linda come home with her. "I'll be there in time to go over everything with you ahead of time."

"Something wrong?" Linda asked when she hung up.

"Jane and Derek are being audited by the IRS. They need me there."

"You do the books?" Aaron asked, sounding as weary as he looked; his eyes were darkly shadowed as though he hadn't slept all night.

"Yes, although we don't have actual books. I do everything on the computer. Did you sleep at all last night?"

"A little." He avoided meeting her eyes.

"I'm glad it's not us," Linda said. "I wouldn't know what to do. Gary does our taxes. I'm sorry you have to go so soon."

"It could work out well, if you come back with me. I'll be busy Tuesday, but we'll have the rest of the week to do things together."

"Are you sure you have to go back? The IRS didn't say so, did they?"

"No, but Jane does need me. I'm responsible for our financial records."

"When are you leaving?" Aaron asked.

"This afternoon. I need time to go over some things tomorrow. I can help you pack, Linda."

"This isn't a good time for me to leave here," Linda said apologetically.

"You don't mean to stay here alone?"

"I'll be fine. There's so much to do before the baby comes."

"You have the rest of the year to get ready."

"Well, Aaron is here...." She looked at him.

"Don't let me stop you."

"No, I really don't want to go home with you, Dawn. The truth is, I'm not afraid. I feel as if all my fear has drained away. I've never felt less concerned about being home alone."

Linda was adamant. Dawn was forced to accept her decision not to visit. If she had to choose between helping her sister or her business partner, Dawn knew the family tie was strongest, but Linda didn't give her a choice. If she wasn't still worried about her sister, she'd be proud of her new-found streak of independence. She wouldn't hear of Dawn missing the IRS appointment.

"I don't need a sitter," she insisted.

Dawn packed, but it didn't take long since most of the clothes she'd brought were dirty and could be stuffed into a plastic garbage bag. She loaded the van, then made one more trip to the big bedroom to check for anything she might have overlooked.

"I'm sorry to see you go." Aaron blocked the doorway, still looking tired and haggard.

"Well, I guess I have everything here." She avoided acknowledging his admission and looked around the bleak old room wishing Linda and Gary had bought a nice cheerful little house in the suburbs.

"I think the watch last night put Linda's mind at ease. She's accepted the idea of a benevolent presence. I can leave without any misgivings about her." He sounded regretful, but the message his eyes were sending had nothing to do with the paranormal.

"I overreacted when you first came. I'm sorry. Linda showed more common sense than I did, calling on an expert to help her. I'm not sure what happened here last night, but I know my sister pretty well. You have put her mind at ease. Thank you for that. Are you leaving soon?"

"Maybe tomorrow. I want to straighten up before I go, and talk to Linda a little more about this. Just so I'm easy in my mind about leaving. There are more facts about the family that might interest her."

She stood some distance away from him, not wanting to touch him by accident. If he wanted to hold her, he had to make that decision himself. She'd made a fool of herself teasing and encouraging him at the roller rink. She didn't know what had gotten into her that night, but it wouldn't happen again.

"Would you mind telling me?" she asked.

If he was surprised by her interest, he didn't show it.

"Carl Junior must have been his mother's darling. Imagine, she had four children and only one lived to be an adult."

She loved listening to the mellow tone of his voice and the careful way he explained things. If this was lecturing, she wanted to be his student—forever.

"Apparently Carl Senior accumulated a lot of money himself, with or without his father-in-law's help. I guess a wealthy father with only one son would have great plans for him, but the family cook had a pretty daughter. It was the 1920s, and young people thought all the old class distinctions were crumbling. Carl Junior thought he could marry the cook's daughter."

"Where did you learn this?"

"I pieced it together by reading all the family history I could find at the library, then going through Louisa's diary again. Some of the things she wrote brought tears to my eyes once I knew the background and realized why she was so unhappy."

His reaction to the sad account made Dawn feel tender toward him.

"Maybe it should be published."

"No, I don't think Louisa would want that. There were pages ripped out, as though they were too painful for her to reread. She liked to keep the family's sorrows a secret."

Dawn held her breath, scarcely believing how real this long-dead family seemed to her now.

"Carl Senior was a tyrant, domineering and possibly abusive. I can only guess what she wrote on the missing pages, but her life must have been hell, always trying to pretend they were a normal, happy family."

"People still do that today, I guess, but then it must have been even worse. What about her family? Her father?"

"Her parents died before Carl Junior was born. She had two sisters, but they apparently followed their husbands to other parts of the country. Louisa inherited a great deal of money, but her husband controlled all of it."

"What else did you learn?"

"Carl Senior must have hated the idea of his son marrying below him—never mind that he was a penniless conniver when he'd manipulated Louisa's father into letting him marry her. There was a brief mention that he'd fired the cook—probably an attempt to get her daughter away from his son."

"That probably made Carl Junior want to marry her even more." It was such a sad, romantic story, she felt weepy.

"Maybe he was stubborn like his father. Maybe they were eloping when they were killed in a car crash. I read the newspaper report on microfilm at the library."

"I never thought of accidents like that happening so long ago. Poor Louisa! What happened to her?"

"I guess she died of a broken heart—helped along by her 'medicinal' doses of bootleg gin she bought from the man who delivered their groceries."

"That's a sad story."

Wonderful and terrible things had happened in the past few days. She didn't know what else to say to Aaron.

"Dawn, are you still up there?"

Dawn heard her sister calling from the bottom of the steps and hurried to the door without looking at Aaron. Maybe they'd said all there was to say.

She tried to tell herself she couldn't wait to go home to the big city. It was worth being challenged by the IRS to get back to the real world. She could deal with audits and antiques and dealers who tried to pawn off reproductions and ruin the mall's reputation. Bad checks, roving swindlers, and people who said, "My grandmother had one," seemed like minor irritations compared to what she'd been through in this idyllic Wisconsin retreat.

She said her goodbyes to Linda in the big kitchen, hugging her just as Aaron walked into the room.

"I'll walk you to your van," he said.

Linda seemed to think this was a good idea. Usually she liked lengthy goodbyes with lots of warnings about safe driving and not getting lost. Today all she said was "Thank you for coming" and "Give me a call so I know you got home all right."

Aaron knew saying goodbye to Dawn was going to be tough; he didn't realize how hard until they were standing by the door of her van.

He cleared his throat, stuck his hands into the pockets of his jeans, and was totally at a loss for words, maybe for the first time in his life.

"Well, I guess this is where I say 'It's been nice knowing you,'" Dawn said, poised to get into the vehicle, not looking at him.

"Has it been?" He took her wrist to delay her, but he still didn't know what he wanted to say.

"Well, it hasn't been boring!" She tried a little too hard to sound jovial; her laugh was short, breathy.

"No, not that." He smiled, still holding her wrist, unconsciously stroking it with his thumb.

"I need one thing before I go," she said.

"Oh?"

"My hand."

"Sorry." He released it, thankful when she didn't move. "Thanks for your help on this."

"I didn't do much."

"You made the time go fast." He smiled, desperately wishing he knew what he wanted. It shouldn't end like this—not when his heart was finally beginning to feel like something more than a hunk of dry ice.

"I had fun at the roller rink," she said. "Sorry you fell."

"No lasting effects." He still had a pain, but it was high up, somewhere under his ribs. He'd just discovered it. "Dawn..."

He hadn't planned to kiss her, but surprise made it all the sweeter. He bent his head and found her lips, wondering how he'd managed to let so much time slip by without taking her in his arms and telling her... telling her...

He couldn't pretend this was a casual goodbye kiss, not when her lips parted under his and blood thundered in his ears.

"Goodbye, Aaron."

This wasn't what he wanted to hear—not so soon, not before...

He kissed her again, slowly, possessively, burying his fingers in silky hair flowing freely over her shoulders and down her back. She wanted his kiss to go on and on, drawing them closer together.

He pulled her against him, sliding his knee between her parted thighs, desperate because he was about to lose something precious.

Suddenly it hurt too much to be so close to Aaron, knowing they were saying goodbye. She didn't want to lose control and admit to feelings that would embarrass him or corner him into saying things he didn't mean.

"Goodbye, Aaron." She pulled away and hurried into the van so he wouldn't see her eyes fill with tears.

He waved as she backed out of the driveway, feeling alone, desolate, unsure of where he'd gone wrong. Somehow he should have found the words, taken the step, forged some kind of link between them.

He felt like a man who'd held a winning lottery ticket and let the wind snatch it away.

Chapter Eight

"I can stay longer, if you want me to," Aaron offered when he was ready to leave.

"No, I feel fine about being here alone," Linda said. "I can't thank you enough for coming."

Later, driving south on Highway 51 to Madison, he had a vague feeling of unease, as though he'd forgotten something or left some important task undone.

The uneasy feeling continued as he carried his luggage and equipment into the foyer of his condo. He'd bought the two-bedroom unit using the assets he'd had left after his divorce, but the sparsely furnished rooms didn't feel like home yet. So far, he hadn't put a single nail hole in the walls or unpacked any of the mementos he'd kept from happier days.

Only the room he used as an office felt as if it belonged to him. He put his equipment on the floor in a corner, adding to the clutter of books and professional journals that overflowed the shelves, then went to the phone and checked his machine for messages.

"Aaron, call me about camping."

A week ago he'd been excited about the trip he and his brother were planning. Now he wasn't sure he wanted to go, but he didn't want to ruin Nathan's vacation plans.

"Well, it's a life," he said, not in the mood to kid himself. It was a good life, in fact, but since meeting Dawn he was starting to question a lot of things. Was he as resigned to loneliness as he'd tried to make himself believe?

He shook his head impatiently and reached for the receiver to begin returning calls, but instead of punching numbers he thought about the time he'd spent with Dawn. She was beautiful and vivacious. He loved her wit, her flashes of insight, her grace and dignity. He admired the way she carried herself, the way she danced on skates, and, yes, even the way she hovered over her sister, sometimes overly protective but obviously loving.

Still holding the phone, he remembered how she blushed when she did something risqué, like patting his behind. Maybe the best of all was watching her pore over the old papers—she was smart and intuitive—knowing how to glean kernels of information without any instruction from him.

Who was he kidding? The very best was holding her in his arms, feeling her lips part and her mouth welcome him. If he really wanted to torture himself, he could visualize her long, sleek legs in shorts, the gentle swell of her breasts, or the way the sun brought out golden glints in her soft brown hair.

He listened halfheartedly to the rest of his messages, his mind leaden with regret. He'd only known the woman a few days during what was, especially for her, a stressful situation.

She'd touched his emotions, made a crack in the protective shell he'd built around himself when his former wife left, but he wasn't ready to open himself to the frustration of a long-distance relationship. Weary and confused, he went into his bedroom and stretched out on the bed, not up to returning any calls just then.

After fighting the heavy weekend traffic, Dawn reached the antique mall just as the last stragglers were being herded out. Even at closing time, it felt like home. While Jane and Derek locked the public entrance, she wandered down the aisles, trying to recharge her energy by enjoying the sparkle of old glassware and the scent of polished wood, but the wonderful relics of past times didn't seem to be working their usual magic. Her mind was still on the disturbing ghost hunter.

Jane caught up with her as she checked to see what had been sold from the stock in their personal space within sight of the checkout counter.

Her partner was tall and willowy, with dark brown hair worn in a tight bun at the back of her neck. She was wearing dark vintage clothes: black velvet toreador pants, and a silk blouse accented by a large art deco style brooch. A dated-but-sophisticated look was her trademark, and her face was striking enough to carry it off. Sometimes she made Dawn feel too ordinary, but they had a partnership made in heaven.

"I'm going to be eternally grateful to you," she told Dawn, "but I feel so guilty calling you back from your vacation."

"It doesn't matter," Dawn assured her. "The big news is Linda's pregnant." She felt an odd restraint, not wanting to talk about things that went bump in the night—or the man who was haunting her heart.

"Welcome home, sweetie." Jane's husband Derek planted a loud kiss on Dawn's cheek and pulled up an overall strap that was slipping off his shoulder. When he wasn't dressed like a corn farmer, he wore shirts that wouldn't stay tucked in and ties that hung above his belt. At six foot six he made Dawn feel like a dwarf, but he was the nicest man she knew.

Dawn needed a Derek in her life, a wholesome, outgoing, dependable man. Maybe if she met someone like him, she could think about the ghost hunter without the pain of wondering if she should have done something differently. Maybe she could start believing in concepts she couldn't see—like trust and love.

"I'm so nervous I can't eat or sleep," said Jane, the cool lady who could walk into a stranger's home and dicker for treasures with the best of the pros.

"Don't worry about the audit," Dawn assured her. "We don't have anything to hide. If we've made mistakes, we'll learn something from the experience."

What had she learned from her mistake—her many mistakes—with Aaron? Their evening at the roller rink was a wonderful memory, but he'd let her leave without...without what? A protest of undying love? The key to his condo? What had she been expecting?

"Crazy!" She'd unintentionally said it out loud, then realized she hadn't been listening to her partner.

"I didn't mean you were crazy! I was just thinking. Let's go over a few things." She wanted to put Jane's mind at ease, even though hers felt as though little balls were whirling around for a lottery drawing in her skull.

The IRS ogre turned out to be a mild-mannered, courteous young woman who went through their operation like the expert accountant she was. Jane and Derek ended up owing $237, but not because of the antique mall. Jane was overjoyed. Dawn wished she could forget about Aaron and feel as happy as she should about their success.

She called Linda every evening for the next few days, then at least twice a week. Gary was home on vacation, and her sister had never sounded happier. She was too excited about decorating the big room as a nursery to even mention what she called her "friendly spirit." They had both decided the front room was much too warm for a baby.

Three weeks after her visit, Linda called her on a Monday evening. "I got a postcard from Aaron," she said. "He was camping in Colorado with his brother. I guess they're into Native American ruins."

It was nice of Aaron to send a postcard to her sister; so why did she feel like a beach ball with all the air squashed out?

She wandered from window to window, but her one-bedroom unit was too small for serious pacing. After changing into running shoes, she went outside and jogged once around the complex, several square blocks of pseudo-Tudor apartment buildings set at random angles. The heat was suffocating, and there was only a tiny whisper of wind blowing in from the west toward Lake Michigan.

Exhausted by the high humidity, she dragged herself up the steps to her second-story apartment. In her imagination, Aaron had been running with her every step of the way, but at least now she understood why the postcard to her sister had been such a shocker. She'd been thinking of him constantly, fantasizing about what might have happened between them. The more she let him into her mind, the less real and more inaccessible he seemed. Linda's postcard made him seem like a flesh-and-blood male again, someone Dawn very much wanted to see.

As she showered she thought about the good things in her life: friends like Jane and Derek, her sister's pregnancy, the

booming success of the antique mall—they were even
thinking of opening a second one farther north. She hadn't
seen Aaron in a few weeks, and she was doing fine. She had
to stop moping over a man who didn't even send her a
postcard.

A shrill ring woke Dawn, but at first she thought it was
part of her dream. Her feet were tangled in the sheet, but she
managed to get her hand on the receiver after nearly
knocking it off the nightstand.

"Hello."

"Dawn, I'm sorry to call so early, but I wanted to catch
you before you went to work."

"What's wrong?" She sat up, still groggy, and read the
luminous numbers on the clock—6:47.

"I think you should come right away!" Linda was crying, her breath coming in harsh sobs.

"Linda, are you all right?"

"Yes. I will be. Can you come?"

"Of course. Just tell me why."

"It's back, Dawn. And this ghost isn't friendly!"

Dawn left her apartment thirty minutes later, headed for
O'Hare.

What was happening in that house? Thinking about it was
making her crazy! It was hard enough to believe she hadn't
imagined Louisa's ghost, but now, flying to her sister's, she
couldn't make sense of anything. Gary was still home, but
Linda sounded more frightened than ever.

After they landed, she walked from the hot runway to the
artificial chill of Central Wisconsin Airport's terminal, not
knowing whether she had the stamina to face the unknown
again. This time she had to resolve the mystery, for her own
peace of mind as well as Linda's. Either that, or persuade

Linda and Gary to sell the house and move. Her sister had been right to call her. What they'd seen together was so bizarre, they both had to experience the new phenomenon for Linda to deal with it. Was Linda a conduit for the paranormal, or could her practical, logical, skeptical sister experience it independently? Dawn still couldn't give up hope that there was some rational explanation.

She rushed blindly through the small terminal, too lost in thought to look around for Linda.

"Dawn!"

She nearly walked into him when he suddenly blocked her way and reached for her duffel.

"Are you all right? You're as white as a sheet."

"Aaron!" How could he be here ahead of her? Did Linda call him first, then ask Dawn as an afterthought?

Her heart was pounding, and her knees were shaky. She'd imagined seeing him again a thousand times, but her fantasies were always set in romantic places: a candle-lit ballroom, a rose-filled garden in the moonlight, a ship at sea under a balmy, tropical sky.

"I'll be fine," she managed to say because he seemed to expect an answer. "I didn't know you were here."

"I wasn't. Linda called me before dawn this morning. She sounded so scared, I drove here right away."

He looked different, and no wonder. He'd shaved his beard but hadn't sacrificed any of his dark, brooding good looks. His chin was strong, his face was bronzed, and his gaze was as mesmerizing as ever. His well-tanned legs were a dark contrast to his white cotton tennis shorts, and his arms were ruddy gold below the sleeves of his light blue shirt. Even though she'd thought of him constantly, she'd forgotten the way his brows arched when he was puzzled. His dark eyes had an inner light that sent liquid heat coursing through her body. When he smiled, he erased all the time they'd spent apart.

"Where's Linda?"

Her sister must expect Aaron to unravel the mystery, but what did Gary think? Did he welcome the presence of a ghost hunter? He was so pragmatic, so self-reliant. It worried her even more to know her brother-in-law felt a need for help.

"At the house. She was beat. She never got back to sleep last night. I offered to pick you up when you called from O'Hare. Was your flight all right?"

"Yes, I guess so. Flying here isn't much faster than driving," she said, not ready to talk about Linda's latest experience. "Not if you count driving to O'Hare, riding on two planes, and driving to Linda's."

"Why didn't you drive?"

"I thought I'd try flying," she answered lamely. "The van needs some work." This was true, even though it hadn't been her main reason for booking a flight. She'd acted mostly on impulse—something she rarely did—in going by plane instead of driving.

Aaron knew the risk he faced in coming back to the Hall house: rekindling his attraction to Dawn. It was no surprise that Linda had called her sister, but he hadn't been prepared for the heady rush of excitement he'd felt when Dawn had walked down the steps from the commuter plane. He'd hurried to the men's room before she saw him and splashed cold water on his face, although it would have done more good lower down. He'd remembered her as beautiful; today she was stunning in a way that made his throat constrict and his palms sweat. This couldn't be happening! He didn't want to mope around like a lovesick adolescent. He didn't want his life complicated.

He also didn't want to let her out of his sight. Carrying her bag to his car, he led the way down the wrong parking lane because he couldn't take his eyes off her.

"Good thing this is CWA instead of O'Hare," he said. "I'd hate to lose my car there."

She didn't trust herself to say anything. Walking beside him, detecting a faint whiff of after-shave and the hot, sun-baked scent of his skin, she was weak with longing. For a few moments it didn't matter why he'd come. She just wanted to be with him.

The Jeep had heated up like an oven in the hot sun, but Aaron ran the air conditioner full-blast until the interior was pleasantly cool.

"The house is hot," he warned, talking about the weather because everything else he wanted to say was too emotionally charged to risk it.

"Too bad Linda doesn't have air yet."

She heard herself talking, but nothing she was saying mattered. Would there ever come a time when she could say how she felt about Aaron?

The ride to Ottawa seemed to take longer than both flights combined, but actually Aaron pulled into the Hall's driveway less than forty-five minutes after her plane landed.

"I'm glad you're here." He hadn't intended to say this, but it slipped out.

"I'm pretty nervous about it." The ghost hunter, not the ghost, was making her feel like a rabbit slated to disappear in a magician's top hat.

"Don't be." His voice was gentle and sincere. "You're safe here with me."

Was she? And what scared her more: the ghost or the ghost hunter? She looked up at the house, wondering if there was some way to determine whether a house was a welcoming place with warm memories or a frightening trap. Linda had loved it on first sight; Gary had been just as enthusiastic. Did they choose the house, or did the house pick them as its next caretakers?

Confused and way out of her league, she shuddered and got out of the Jeep.

Linda rushed down the porch steps and flew into Dawn's arms, blinking back tears when she was through hugging. "I'm so glad you're here."

"Tell me everything right away."

"I've told Aaron—" She stopped, possibly because she read the worried look in Dawn's eyes. "It was much much worse, like someone going berserk, throwing things."

"Really throwing things?" Dawn felt an inner chill that had nothing to do with the temperature.

"Not in the sense that anything was moved, but the noise was terrifying. I would have died if Gary hadn't been here and heard it, too."

"Let's go inside," Aaron said.

His suggestion made sense, but Dawn resented it. Didn't he think they had enough sense to come in out of the heat? Did he believe the Girard sisters were imbeciles? Was he secretly mocking them, silently laughing at their fear? She bit back an angry response, slowly realizing that she wanted a target—any target—for her overcharged emotions. She was being overly sensitive and needed to calm down.

"I made sandwiches and lemonade," Linda said. "I've definitely been eating for two." Dawn had no appetite, but thinking of her sister's condition helped her get hold of her emotions. She wasn't angry at anyone—only terribly upset that her sister's life was being turned topsy-turvy again.

"Good, I'm starved," Aaron said. "Where should I put this bag?"

"Put it in the downstairs bedroom," Linda said. "Dawn won't want to sleep upstairs after she hears what happened."

Chapter Nine

Gary came in the back way and met them in the living room, quickly walking over and giving his sister-in-law a big hug.

"Thanks for coming, Dawn. You were in on this before, so we were sure you would want to know what's going on. We're counting on Dr. Mead to psych this out for us."

The big, rusty-haired man nodded at Aaron, surprising Dawn by the deference he showed him. It wasn't like her brother-in-law to relinquish control over anything, but he seemed to be depending on the ghost hunter for a solution.

"Do you need anything?" she asked Linda, worried about her sister's pallid skin. "Water, something stronger?"

"No, thanks. I'm all right now. But, Dawn, it was bad. I've never had such a scare, much worse than the first time, and Gary was here with me. Tell her what happened, honey. I can hardly stand to think about it."

Gary bent over, kissed his wife's forehead, and patted her arm in the subdued manner of a funeral parlor visitor. If he was this grim, Linda must have been terrified!

"What happened?" Dawn urged.

"Nothing I ever heard before," her brother-in-law said. "We were asleep—had been for a long time—when it started. It sounded like someone was trying to smash every stick of wood in the place."

"Was anything really broken?"

"Nothing—and nothing was moved either. I checked the whole house, inside and out. I couldn't see anything to explain the noise. It would've taken a wrecking ball to create havoc like we heard."

"I'd already told Gary everything that happened while he was gone," Linda said. "Until last night, he was sure we'd imagined seeing Louisa."

"I didn't buy the ghost stuff," he admitted, "but I've never heard anything like that din—not even in a factory full of machines all going at once. It was like a noise exploding inside my brain." He protectively put his hand on Linda's shoulder. "She didn't have to talk me into calling both of you. I don't have any answers."

Aaron was rubbing his face—his sun-bronzed, shaven face. Dawn had imagined him without his beard, but she'd never suspected that the sight of his strong jaw and lean cheeks would make her heart do flip-flops. She loved the tiny cleft in his chin and the way his ears were flat against his head with wisps of dark hair curling over the edges. As frightening as Gary's story was, she couldn't keep her eyes from straying to Aaron's serious face.

"The noise wasn't the worst of it," Linda said. "It went on so long we were ready to get out of the house, but afterward, the silence was horrible. Not quiet like the countryside around here. This sounds melodramatic, but the only word I can think of to describe it is evil."

"A preternatural silence," Aaron said, liking the situation less and less. He'd heard the Halls's story when he'd arrived, but instead of growing calmer, Linda seemed to be getting more agitated.

"What's that?" Dawn asked.

"An inexplicable quietness. A psychic absence of all sound. Usually people who experience it feel a malevolent presence. They may feel watched."

"That's exactly it!" Linda agreed, her cheeks unnaturally flushed as her agitation grew.

"I'll be honest with you, Aaron," her husband said. "When Linda told me what happened here, I had you pegged as a phony. It wouldn't be hard for an expert to rig that show with the rocker."

"Then why call me now?"

Aaron didn't seem offended, but Dawn could feel the intensity of his interest, like the way summer air feels before an electrical storm.

"Electronics are my game, but I couldn't find a trace of anything suspicious. You could have removed the evidence, but it would be hard to tamper with this house without leaving something I'd pick up on. I went over it with a fine-tooth comb. The President could visit, it's so clean. Then I called some people I knew in the service."

"Gary was in army intelligence," Linda explained.

"Better the feds than the university," Aaron said dryly. "I do like my job."

"The bottom line is," Gary said, "I'm ready to get rid of the house rather than have Linda go through anything like that again. But we're sure willing to give you another go at it, Aaron."

"Selling the house won't solve the problem," Linda said, clinging to Gary's arm as though she needed the support. "What if a family with children bought it, and they had to go through what I've experienced? I'd feel so guilty. Anyway, this is our home, and I love it. We've started decorating the nursery, and I don't want to give it up. Our child should be able to chase butterflies in the yard and catch fireflies at night. We have room here for Simba and Lucky and seven other pets if we want them."

"God forbid!" Gary said, putting his arm around her shoulders and hugging her against him. "Anyway, I've decided to take Linda to a motel in Wausau for the night. I can come back if you want me here, but no way is she going through something like that again."

"That's probably a good idea," Aaron said. "I think you should stay there with her, Gary, if it's all right with you, Dawn?"

She was surprised to find herself with a decision to make. Of course she wanted Linda away from whatever was happening, but was it a good idea for her to stay alone all night with Aaron? Her mind was in low gear. Even as she'd flown there on the plane, she'd nurtured a tiny hope of finding a logical explanation for everything. But Gary sounded ready to give up. If her clear-minded, physics-oriented brother-in-law was spooked, how could she grasp at straws and hope the situation was only a bad dream? At least he didn't have any doubts about Aaron's intentions. But did that mean she could trust the ghost hunter in the dark hours of a late-night vigil?

Gary smiled a little sheepishly, making her realize she did have to say something.

"Yes, stay with Linda," she said woodenly to her brother-in-law.

"I can stay here alone," Aaron offered, holding his breath in the irrational hope that Dawn wouldn't take him up on the offer. Having her here would accomplish nothing, but he had a hunch that the next time they said goodbye, it would be for good. He wasn't ready for that.

"I guess I can stay." She had enough misgivings to send her hitchhiking back to Chicago, but something had happened to her in this house. She couldn't bail out without reaching some kind of a conclusion.

Before Gary left with Linda, he drew Dawn aside, giving her another chance to change her mind about staying. They were alone together in the master bedroom on the pretext of packing an overnight bag for Linda while she rested downstairs for a while.

"I can see why Linda doesn't want to give up on the house," she said, looking around at the cheerful room with its satiny white and Wedgwood blue wallpaper and newly revarnished, honey-tan floors.

Gary efficiently stuffed some socks into a duffel.

"I thought it was all in her head," he admitted bluntly, "especially after I checked out Mead. But after last night, I'm not sure of anything."

"Whose idea was it to call me?" In the confusing muddle of possibilities, this was one fact that could be confirmed.

"Mine. You're so levelheaded, I thought you could help—somehow. I wasn't thinking so straight, I guess. Now that you're here, I don't feel at all easy about leaving you in the house. Maybe you should come with us. You don't need to stay here. I've just about made up my mind about putting this place on the market."

"If nothing happens when Linda isn't here..."

"It could still happen again when she is here. You know how much I travel. I can't leave her here alone if..."

"If something about her is making it happen?" She knew how hard it was for Gary to admit anyone could be psychic, especially his own wife. She could see the agony her practical, sensible brother-in-law was going through.

"Yeah, but dragging you here is seeming like a worse idea all the time."

"No, I want to find out what's going on."

She clenched her fists, sure of her decision but shaken by the intensity of her need to see it through. Was it because of Aaron, or did she have to face this for the sake of her own mental well-being? Either way, she'd never made a harder decision, one that frightened and excited her at the same time.

A short while later she and Aaron stood on the front porch, watching through the screen as Gary and Linda drove away.

Outside the sun cut through the leafy canopy around the house and formed simmering patches of heat on the yellow-green lawn. It was hot, but Dawn shivered and hugged her arms across her chest. She felt like a caged bird flapping its wings against bars, longing for freedom to fly away.

"It's good to see you," he said.

"I... Thank you."

She wanted to respond in a way that would let him know how much she'd missed him, but everything that came to mind seemed too banal or too revealing.

"I'd like to go over the upstairs one more time, then maybe catch a nap. It could be a long night," he said.

"What do you think will happen? Do you think we'll experience the same thing Linda and Gary heard?"

"I wish I knew. Come upstairs with me."

The big bedroom where Dawn had slept was so changed she hardly recognized it. The ceiling was a soft white, and cuddly puppies and kittens frolicked on newly hung cream-colored wallpaper.

"Where's the bed?" she asked.

"In the storage room. Gary couldn't get it down the stairway without cutting it in two."

"They bought a new rocker." She sat in the high-backed maple chair and rocked it gently, not liking the creak on the bare boards of the floor.

"They've ordered carpeting," Aaron said, as if reading her mind.

"There's nothing spooky about this room now, only it needs more furniture for the baby. Where's the old rocker?"

"Gary carried it out to the storage shed in back."

"He probably didn't want to keep it around after he heard about the manifestation. Maybe he thought it would trigger Linda's imagination." In spite of what all three of them had witnessed, she didn't want Aaron to think she was blindly accepting the whole paranormal business.

Pacing restlessly from window to window, she didn't need to be psychic to sense Aaron's eyes on her.

"Are you going to bring the old rocker back here?" she asked with misgivings.

"I've thought about it," he admitted. "But not tonight. I want things to be just as they were when Linda and Gary heard the racket."

"I'm only doing this for one night," she warned.

"Dawn, don't stay if you're frightened. I don't want you to suffer."

Didn't he know her whole life was a disaster since she'd met him? She didn't know what to feel or what to believe.

He couldn't stop staring at her, wondering how he'd forgotten the way she squared her shoulders when she was agitated. She had an elusive quality, a fragile beauty that didn't quite mask her inner strength. He felt protective of her, but he also responded to her independence.

"I'm staying. Do you think Linda has to be here for anything to happen?"

"I'm not going to speculate," he said more gruffly than he intended. He wanted to be able to give her answers, satisfying explanations that would erase the frown on her brow. But he had to remember that she didn't trust ghost hunters—or men, and he fit both categories. He had no way of knowing her real reason for coming. Was she still suspicious of his motives? Was she doing her duty as a big sister? Had seeing the manifestation changed her, or was she there as his watchdog?

"I'm going to sack out on the couch," he said, deciding there was nothing he had to do right away.

"I see you brought your machines," she said, following him into the hallway and down the stairs.

"Yes, I might get some readings. So far, modern technology has pretty much failed me, but I have everything on a wheeled cart this time. If a manifestation lasts as long as it did for Linda and Gary, I may be able to zero in on it."

Her insides felt frozen into a block of ice, and she recognized her distress for what it was: dread at the thought of Aaron pursuing some demonic force with his gadgets and cords.

Although she didn't know how he could relax under the circumstances, he stretched out on the living room couch, leaving her to her own devices. A few minutes later she heard the rhythmic breathing that told her he was sleeping.

Aaron awoke after a few hours of fitful napping, feeling as hot and rumpled as though he'd worn his clothes for a week. Dawn was nowhere in sight, so he took a quick shower and dressed in jeans and a white shirt. He was as ready for the vigil as he would ever be.

He looked for Dawn and saw her tossing a stick for the dog in the backyard. He wanted to join her, but he wasn't sure how to approach her. In spite of all that had happened, did she still mistrust him? The tension between them angered him, but it also made him miserable.

She ran toward the woods, her hair tinged with gold in the sun, and his chest ached with longing. He hoped she'd see him standing on the back steps and come toward him, but she was engrossed in her game with Lucky. He went back into the house, not sure what would happen between them after their night watch. He was beginning to feel like a cricket stuck on a glue trap; he might be able to pull away, but he was sure to leave part of himself behind.

Dawn went inside when she caught a glimpse of Aaron retreating into the house, but the rest of the afternoon passed with only desultory conversation. They shared a makeshift cold supper, but neither of them had an appetite.

"I'm going for a walk," she said, not knowing how long she could stand the stalemate between them.

"I'll come with you."

He didn't care whether she wanted him along. His scalp felt prickly with anticipation; he seemed to be treading on a path of sliding gravel toward a bottomless drop-off. Nothing—not his oral exams for his doctorate, not Hell Night when he joined his fraternity, certainly not his paranormal investigations—had ever made him this jumpy. He didn't want to let Dawn out of his sight.

The sky was clouding over, and by tacit agreement they didn't go far from the house. The humidity made Aaron's shirt stick to his back, and Dawn pulled her pink T-shirt out of the waistband of her shorts, feeling as hot as she had at midday. The headache that had begun as a twinge over her left eye in late afternoon had intensified and crept down to her cheek, throbbing like a toothache.

They went back and watched the storm clouds gather from the front porch, sitting at the far ends of the glider. Dawn went inside for a cola, hoping the caffeine would ease her "weather headache," then came back out for lack of anything else to do. She stared at the dark strip of road and a thick grove of trees beyond it, the pine needles black under an ominous sky, and had never felt so desolate.

The storm broke with jagged streaks of lightning ripping across the distant sky, and in her soul it felt like darkest midnight.

"When should we go upstairs?"

"Now, I think. Sitting on a metal glider in a lightning storm is a lot riskier than anything we'll see or hear tonight. I hope you believe that you're not in any danger from the paranormal, Dawn."

His voice caressed her name, and for a moment she almost hoped...

The rain began in torrential gusts, and they ran around checking windows, stopping to comfort Lucky in the mudroom where they'd put him because Dawn remembered he was afraid of storms.

The last room they checked was the nursery.

"I was scared of storms when I was a kid," he said softly. "I crawled under my bed quite a few times until I was old enough to understand my dad's lectures on upper air disturbances."

"Then you weren't afraid anymore?" She hunched her shoulders, wishing the night was over.

"Yeah, I still was, so I found excuses to be in the basement whenever a big one hit."

Standing behind her, he put his arms all the way around her, holding her against him until she could feel courage flowing from his body to hers. For a moment she forgot

Linda's experiences, forgot storms and ghosts, and only wanted him to hold her.

He nuzzled her hair, losing himself in the delicate scent, and his spine tingled when she relaxed against him.

She could hear his breathing and feel the warm tickle of air when he pushed her hair away from her ear. When a violent bolt of lightning crackled over the treetops, she jumped but stayed in the circle of his arms, snuggling even closer when he ran his fingertips over the back of her neck.

The room was black except when an electrical display lit the sky, and she didn't have the will to resist when he pressed his hands against her midsection and slowly moved them upward until he was gently cupping her breasts.

"I missed you," he whispered in her ear.

Lightning struck so near it seemed to bounce off the metal fencing around Lucky's kennel. Aaron murmured something comforting, but his words were drowned out by a boom of thunder.

How could something be so wrong and so right at the same time? He could feel the faint trembling in her body, and he wanted her all the more because of it. He yearned for her to need him. He moved his hands under her shirt, stroking her through the satin of her bra.

"Do you trust me, Dawn?"

She didn't know how to answer. She felt like mercury under his touch, breaking apart into bits and flowing back together as he relentlessly caressed her breasts, flattening them under his palms, reforming them between his fingers, stealing her breath and her will.

"I…"

His mouth was hot on the back of her neck, and her knees turned to gelatin.

"Do you?"

"I can't think when you're doing that." Did he know the effect he was having on her?

He took his hands away. "I didn't know my question was so difficult."

"I know you won't hurt me, Aaron," she quickly assured him.

"Should I be grateful that you're not afraid of me?"

"No! You're twisting things. You can't expect me to be easy in my mind about . . ."

Her attempt to explain was more painful than a direct denial. "I'll find some chairs," he said curtly, leaving the room.

What would have happened if Gary hadn't moved the bed? His lips burned; his groin throbbed. He'd never felt so out of control. He wanted her more than he wanted his next breath of air, but one thing hadn't changed: love didn't work without trust.

She hadn't lied to him; he supposed he should be grateful for that. But gratitude didn't take away the hurt.

She pressed her forehead to the cool glass of the window, indifferent to the storm still raging outside. She was in a haunted house with a ghost hunter, and all she could think of was how it would feel to lie naked in Aaron's arms, to cushion her cheek on his broad chest, to entwine her legs around his and give in to the passion that sizzled between them like the lightning outside the window.

She'd been desperately close to that moment of surrender, but he'd demanded something she couldn't give: an avowal of trust. She was trapped in a bizarre nightmare, wanting nothing more than to end the ghastly ghost business with a logical, natural explanation. But even Gary couldn't find a rational solution. Was Aaron involved? What did she know about him, about his obsession with the paranormal? The things she knew about him as a man should have made her fall willingly into his arms—or flee.

She sucked in her breath, and her ribs ached from the tension.

"You can still back out. Take my car and go to a motel." He stood in the doorway, dragging the air mattress behind him.

"No, I don't think I can."

"This is the best thing I found to sit on." He threw it on the floor against the wall where the bed had stood. "I'll round up some pillows."

She couldn't imagine trying to sleep, but that wasn't his intention. He sat on one side of the mattress, pushing a couple of pillows behind his back, and gave her a pair to do the same.

The storm was moving away, but night darkened the room. The hall light was on, and he'd moved his equipment just inside the door.

Dawn got up to open the windows, gasping for air in the humid closeness of the upper story. No sooner had she opened it than the temperature plummeted in the wake of the storm. She shivered and retreated from the window, lowering herself to the mattress to wait with Aaron.

They sat with their backs against the wall, not talking at all. Tense from waiting, Dawn was hit with a wave of weariness so draining she felt limp. Her arms were cold, and she hugged herself, curling up on the end of the mattress and wondering how she would get through the night that had hardly begun.

She was exhausted, but her eyes were wide open. Minutes passed, then hours, and it seemed as if they'd waited a dozen hours for something that wasn't going to happen. Only an occasional rustle told her Aaron was awake, too. The thunder was far distant now, and the rain had slowed to a steady pitter-patter. She didn't purposely resist sleep, but she stayed alert, hearing all the tiny night sounds of the old house.

It was the hardest thing he'd ever done, keeping her at arm's length when every molecule in his body was screaming to touch her. The scent of her hair made him giddy with longing, and every soft breath she took echoed in his consciousness. Was this some self-imposed trial, or only an exercise in self-torture? He'd always felt handicapped in his investigations because he wasn't a psychic; he didn't seem to have any of the sensitivity of the people who reported paranormal activities. This made him an objective, fair-minded investigator, but it also made him a perpetual outsider. He wanted to come in from the cold void where he was only a spectator. He wanted more than life had offered him so far, but he was afraid he and Dawn could never break down the invisible wall between them.

Suddenly all hell broke loose. Sound exploded like rockets over a battlefield, and Dawn screamed in terror. The windows threatened to explode inward; the boards in the floor crackled like a burning forest; every timber in the room resounded as though a thousand crowbars were being pounded on the walls.

Aaron grabbed Dawn and held her tight against him, trying to make a safe haven in his arms.

"It's here," he whispered urgently, fighting his own unexpected fear as he struggled to comfort her.

Chapter Ten

"I know you're in pain," Aaron said as he cradled Dawn's head against his chest. "But you're not alone anymore."

His words penetrated Dawn's fear, and she struggled against the panic gripping her.

"Let me help you. I care about you, Louisa."

Dawn couldn't believe it! He wasn't talking to her! She could hear his words clearly over the unearthly din filling the room, and he was talking to the ghost.

"It is you, isn't it, Louisa? I'm sorry for your grief. You've suffered too much for too long a time."

The room was filled with a clatter like the banging of an iron spoon on wooden shutters, but Dawn sensed a slight lowering of the volume, a lessening of intensity.

"L-Louisa?" she stammered, trying to reconcile what she was hearing with the peaceful image of a mother and child in a rocker.

"Let go of your pain, Louisa," Aaron urged. "I know it hurts, but it's time to move beyond grief."

"Are you sure it's not Carl?" Dawn whispered against his ear, getting up enough nerve to sit upright and look around the room.

"It's a possibility," he whispered, "but I sure hope not."

Wind seemed to howl through the room, and the clatter rose in volume again when Aaron diverted his attention to Dawn.

"Help me," he whispered to her, squeezing her hand so hard she could feel his anxiety.

"Louisa," she said, barely able to choke out the name. Surely her weak voice couldn't be heard over the unholy racket filling the room, but she couldn't believe she'd said the name.

"Louisa," Aaron begged, "listen to me. I'm your friend."

"I want to be your friend, too, Louisa," Dawn said, dredging her voice up from her midsection.

"Have you come to rock your babies, Louisa? It's a terrible thing when little ones die so young. You've suffered more than anyone should. I feel your pain, Louisa. I want to take it away from you."

Dawn heard something she could hardly endure: a cry of pure pain so deep and unrelieved it went beyond agony and suffering.

"The chair isn't here anymore. Is that why your pain is raging out of control, Louisa? Because you can't comfort yourself in the rocker? Did you hold your babies there as they breathed their last? I'm sorry for your pain, Louisa," Aaron said. "Please, let me help you."

Dawn could feel Aaron's arm trembling against hers. Had he meant what he'd said about the paranormal never hurting people? Was he afraid for their sakes or only so intent on helping the tormented soul that he was shaking from the effort? She squeezed his arm and realized she was trembling too.

"Are you angry because your chair is gone, Louisa?" she asked, her voice sounding faint and far away. "No one meant to hurt you by taking it away."

The room became ominously quiet, and Dawn felt woozy enough to faint. She felt what Linda had described: a malevolent presence far worse than the noisy spirit.

"I said something wrong," she gasped, holding on to Aaron for dear life.

"No, you didn't," he whispered, hoping he was right. "You're doing fine."

She wanted to believe him, but she'd never been so frightened.

"Louisa, no one meant to hurt you. These are good people living in your house now. They're going to have a baby of their own. Can you see the new chair? It's here because there's going to be a new baby to rock. Your chair is gone, Louisa, because it's time for you to move on. You deserve peace. The little ones you love are waiting for you. Don't cling to this place. Push aside your pain, Louisa. You can do it. Move beyond it. We love you, Louisa. We don't want you to suffer anymore."

"Your babies are waiting," Dawn echoed. "Go to them."

Please, please, please, go! she thought, not sure she could survive much more of the unholy silence.

"We're here to take your pain away from you, Louisa. You're free to move on," Aaron called out more loudly.

Dawn didn't know if the dots of light she saw were real, or if she was on the verge of losing consciousness. The only reality in her world was Aaron's arm across her shoulders, his icy hand on her arm.

Dawn shivered uncontrollably, and Aaron felt helpless, only able to offer the cold comfort of holding her. He was taking a terrible risk, one he hadn't expected. If this wasn't Louisa's spirit, he was up against some force he'd never dreamed of opposing—never even admitted its existence. Hundreds of cases pointed to Louisa as the source of the disturbances, but the room was a seething mass of hostility. She'd seemed so benign in the last manifestation. What if Carl was there, ready to wreak vengeance for the loss of his only living son? What if the patriarch had been an insane brute, murdering his own offspring? Too much about the man had been concealed behind the stylized accounts of his family.

"Louisa, give us a sign if you're here. I understand that you're angry because your chair is gone. Please forgive us and put aside your anger," he begged, so frightened for Dawn's sake that he was ready to try anything.

Did ghosts ever do what you wanted them to? Dawn didn't know, but she did hear fear in Aaron's voice. It aroused a protective urge so overwhelming she actually pulled away from him and rose to her feet.

"Dawn!"

"Louisa, you're dead, and you should go away now! You're hurting yourself, and you're hurting other people. My sister wants to live in this lovely home with her new baby, but you're scaring her too much. Your chair is gone. It's in the shed, but you don't need it anymore. You should be ashamed of yourself! Your babies are waiting on the other side, and you'll go to them if you're any kind of mother at all! We're sorry for you. We know you hurt something terrible, but use your love for your babies to go on."

"My God," Aaron said, leaping up and taking her in his arms.

She thought she'd done something awful, but the malevolence that surrounded them seemed to dissolve. She'd never felt such an odd feeling: relief and peace mingled with fear of believing.

Dawn crumpled to her knees, and Aaron tried to cover her body with his, but suddenly he knew she wasn't in any danger.

"I can't believe I did that," she gasped, too shaken to focus on what was happening in front of them.

"Look," he said urgently, gesturing at the total darkness of the room.

The beam from the hallway was gone.

"Electrical storm...we must have blown the circuits," she said.

"Never mind that—look over there, darling."

She blinked her eyes, slowly beginning to see the dim outline of a figure, the light emanating from it so faint that it had no more substance than a smear on a pane of glass.

Darling! Aaron had called her darling!

"It's best that you go on, Louisa," he urged in a soothing whisper. "You don't want to hurt anyone. You deserve peace now. You can do it, Louisa."

The shape took on a stronger glow, and Dawn could see the outline of a painfully forlorn-looking woman in a long dress, her shapeless garment hanging on a thin frame. Then the luminance that gave definition to the figure blurred, and only a column of light remained, a green fluorescent shaft that hovered in midair.

Dawn discovered hot tears on her cheeks, and only Aaron's arm around her kept her from weeping hysterically.

"It's moving," he said.

Aaron's voice gave her the courage to follow the light with her eyes as it slowly moved toward the doorway to the hall.

She nearly collapsed in relief when it vanished from sight, but Aaron walked to the door, taking her with him in the security of his arm.

"We need to follow."

He was right. They'd come this far. They had to see it through.

The glow was brighter now, filling the open doorway to the master bedroom.

"Is she looking for her rocker?" Dawn whispered, not expecting an answer.

The room ahead of them seemed to shimmer with a peachy glow. They watched awestruck as the column of light broke up into a whole spectrum of colors like a miniature rainbow on an oil spill. Then it passed through the windows at the back of the house and left the room in blackness.

Aaron threw up the sash over the window seat and crawled out onto the balcony, giving Dawn his hand to pull her through. The tarred surface underfoot was slippery, and rainwater had accumulated in small puddles on the uneven surface.

Without the light of moon or stars, Aaron had to strain to see the shed at the back of the lot.

"Is she going to the shed for the rocker?" Dawn asked, reading his thoughts.

"I don't think so." He was afraid to be optimistic, but the light was rising, moving faster since it had left the confines of the house.

Dawn watched awestruck as the glow fragmented. Then, in a burst that seemed to flash inside her head, it was gone.

Aaron walked over to the edge of the balcony and rested his hand on the flaky, painted surface of the old railing.

Imagining that he might fall through the flimsy barrier of aged wood, she bounded toward him, forgetting that heights made her nervous. She reached out her hands and was swept into his arms with the force of a summer squall.

His mouth was warm and tantalizing, caressing her lips
with the gentleness due the fragile petals of a blossom. She
shivered with excitement, reaching up and putting her hands
on his bare shoulders, loving the firm swell of muscle under his smooth skin.

Her touch was like a magic wand, sending sparks of desire through his body. He held her against him, wanting to
absorb her, to meld with the sensuous softness of her lithe
form. He brushed her eyelids with his lips, feeling the dainty
tickle of her lashes and inhaling the intoxicating scent of her
skin.

His hands rested lightly on her waist, then slowly stroked
the swell of her hips and the sleek lines of her thighs. Her
moan of pleasure mingled with his deep sigh, and he spread
his hands over her bottom, lifting her against him with all
the passion he'd locked up with his doubts.

Their mouths came together with a rush of urgency, and
she didn't think she'd ever been kissed before, not like this,
not with the sweet fury of a hive of hungry bees, not by a
man who could make her crazy with love.

Her lips parted under his, and he kissed her with blind
urgency, terrified because there were so many things to say.
But when her tongue touched his in invitation, he responded with all his stored-up yearning.

He tasted wonderful; he felt wonderful! His kisses were
sweet beyond imagining; his lips covered hers with an urgency that filled all the empty places in her heart.

"Aaron," she gasped, trembling in the circle of his arms
and regretting every moment they'd wasted because a ghost
stood between them. "Can we forget about the thing that
happened here?"

"Forget it! My darling, I'll remember the way you stood
up to Louisa until my dying day. You were magnificent—
unbelievable!"

My darling. Those two words made the fear and horror forgettable. She wrapped her arms around him and buried her face against his chest, trembling in reaction to all that had happened.

"You're shivering. You've had a terrible shock." He held her against him for another moment of delirious pleasure, then let himself be ruled by concern for her. "I've got to get you warm."

"As if you weren't!"

He kissed her forehead and led her toward the window, stepping through first to better help her climb down from the window seat.

"If this were my house, I'd put in a sliding-glass door so I could carry you out to sleep under the stars," he murmured into her hair as he again held her tight, trying to still her trembling.

To sleep under the stars—together! For such a long time she'd been afraid to hope for happiness like this, but now the desertion of her father and her canceled wedding seemed like memories stored on the fading pages of an aged scrapbook. "To sleep under the stars," she whispered in a dreamy daze.

He left her for only an instant, hurrying to the duffel he'd left in his bedroom. When he returned, he draped a cotton-knit sweater around her shoulders and guided her down the steps in the dark, carefully feeling his way.

"I'll find the circuit breaker and get the power back on, then make you something warm."

"No, not yet," she begged, not ready to let him go so far from her.

"Can we sit on the porch for a while?" she asked almost shyly.

He'd pulled an afghan off the couch as they'd walked through the living room and wrapped the stretchy yarn blanket around her as they stood on the porch, using it to pull her close to him.

Her lips were warmer now, soft and yielding under his urgent kiss, and he bent his head to trail his lips over the surface of her throat.

He was so elated he couldn't think straight. A contaminated house was clean again; the Halls could get on with their lives and know they would raise their child in a wholesome, loving atmosphere. It was enough to make him joyous, but he was more than that. He was delirious with love, wanting to put the pieces of his own life together in a meaningful new way.

"Oh, Aaron." She hugged him tightly, knowing she would never walk away from him again. "We got off to such a bad start."

"It doesn't matter. We can start over now. I don't want to live without you," he said.

She held her breath, afraid to believe what he was saying because she so badly wanted it to be true.

"Is this really happening? Can we be this happy?"

"Believe it," he said. "Can you forgive me for doubting your trust?"

"You were right. I didn't trust you. I didn't trust anything I couldn't see, hold, measure...."

"You trusted me when I said a paranormal experience couldn't hurt you. It was you who convinced Louisa to pass over."

"I was afraid!"

"So was I. You trusted me when I was talking to Louisa's spirit."

"You sounded so compassionate—so eager to comfort her. The least I could do was help you. I'm beginning to accept a whole lot of things on faith."

She didn't know if Aaron could completely forgive her for opposing all his early efforts, but her heart was singing with joy for the love she heard in his voice.

"You only showed good sense. You're not the first skeptic to wonder why I like to look through paranormal keyholes." He nuzzled her hair, so full of things he wanted to say to her that his heart felt swollen.

"I'm going to have doubts in the morning," she said with a light, self-conscious laugh that made his spine tingle. "Not about you," she added when she saw the stricken look on his face. "I'm going to stew over it and try to explain away Louisa's ghost. But I won't be able to, will I?"

"The important thing is putting it behind us. I love you, Dawn. I love you so very much." He kissed her eyelids and rubbed his nose against hers, wanting each caress to make an indelible impression on her consciousness.

"I love you, too. Oh, Aaron, I do love you! I don't care if you want to chase Bigfoot or fish for the Loch Ness Monster. I want to be part of everything that's important to you."

"Nothing has ever been as important to me as you are." He held her tight, covering her mouth with his and burying his fingers in her silky hair.

She let the afghan drop, and his sweater fell off her shoulders, but she wasn't cold—not anymore. Aaron's arms were warm and strong, holding her against him with heart-rending tenderness.

He led her to the glider and pulled her down on his lap without relinquishing her lips, kissing her again and again as the chains squeaked in rhythm to their swinging.

"Will you marry me?" he asked, not believing how nervous he felt about her answer. Was their closeness an illusion, or was something incredible beginning here? "It's a for-better-or-for-worse proposition. I never plan to have a hundred-dollar-an-hour practice or own more than two suits.''

"I'll buy all your clothes at rummage sales, and we'll spend our vacations tracking down Abe Lincoln's spirit.''

"Does that mean yes?''

"Yes, yes, yes!'' She put her arms around his neck and pulled his face to hers, raining little kisses on his brow, his cheeks, even the tip of his nose.

Then she was on her back, a little dizzy from the unceasing sway of the glider, with Aaron leaning over her in the dark, his hand behind her head and his lips locked on hers.

Time stood still, and she couldn't believe happiness like this was possible. The rightness of loving Aaron made her giddy, and she put her arms around his neck, pulling him even closer.

Loving Dawn was a revelation; holding her was so satisfying to his soul that making her happy became his only goal in life.

The new day took him by surprise, the first faint light of morning washing over Dawn's flushed cheeks and bright eyes. He could hold her in his arms for an eternity and not tire of her sweetness, tenderness, and love.

They walked to the screen, looking across the road at the dark silhouette of the woods without any of the evening's sense of menace.

"Will this be a commuter's marriage?'' he asked, holding her away from him, looking passionate and happy and concerned all at the same time. "I know how much your business means to you, but I do have tenure and ghost-hunting profs aren't in high demand on the job market.''

"Jane and I have talked about opening a second mall farther north. I think Madison might be the perfect place for it.''

"I don't want you to give up a business that means a lot to you."

"I won't be. I'll be giving Jane and me a chance to make it on our own, and we'll still be partners."

"I'm crazy about you." He kissed her again, and she didn't understand how each kiss could seem even more wonderful than the one before it, when every one was perfectly delightful.

In the mudroom Lucky woke up and barked like the squirrel-chasing hound he was, but the house behind them was tranquilly quiet, so peaceful they were drawn inside.

"I'll call Linda and tell her she can come home."

"Great, but—not quite so quickly, darling....

* * * * *

JINGLE BELLS, WEDDING BELLS:
Silhouette's Christmas Collection for 1994

Christmas Wish List

*To beat the crowds at the malls and get the perfect present for *everyone*, even that snoopy Mrs. Smith next door!

*To get through the holiday parties without running my panty hose.

*To bake cookies, decorate the house and serve the perfect Christmas dinner—just like the women in all those magazines.

*To sit down, curl up and read my Silhouette Christmas stories!

Join *New York Times* bestselling author Nora Roberts, along with popular writers Barbara Boswell, Myrna Temte and Elizabeth August, as we celebrate the joys of Christmas—and the magic of marriage—with

JINGLE BELLS, WEDDING BELLS

Silhouette's Christmas Collection for 1994.

JBWB

MILLION DOLLAR SWEEPSTAKES (III)

No purchase necessary. To enter, follow the directions published. Method of entry may vary. For eligibility, entries must be received no later than March 31, 1996. No liability is assumed for printing errors, lost, late or misdirected entries. Odds of winning are determined by the number of eligible entries distributed and received. Prizewinners will be determined no later than June 30, 1996.

Sweepstakes open to residents of the U.S. (except Puerto Rico), Canada, Europe and Taiwan who are 18 years of age or older. All applicable laws and regulations apply. Sweepstakes offer void wherever prohibited by law. Values of all prizes are in U.S. currency. This sweepstakes is presented by Torstar Corp., its subsidiaries and affiliates, in conjunction with book, merchandise and/or product offerings. For a copy of the Official Rules governing this sweepstakes offer, send a self-addressed, stamped envelope (WA residents need not affix return postage) to: MILLION DOLLAR SWEEPSTAKES (III) Rules, P.O. Box 4573, Blair, NE 68009, USA.

SWP-S1094

SILHOUETTE®

Desire®

ANNETTE BROADRICK'S
SONS OF TEXAS
SERIES CONTINUES

Available in October from Silhouette Desire,
TEMPTATION TEXAS STYLE! (SD #883) is the latest
addition to Annette Broadrick's series about the
Callaway family.

Roughed-up rodeo cowboy Tony Callaway thought
women were nothing but trouble—but once this
lonesome cowboy took one look into Christina
O'Reilly's sultry green eyes, he was sure to change
his mind!

Don't miss Tony Callaway's story in TEMPTATION
TEXAS STYLE! by Annette Broadrick, Desire's MAN OF
THE MONTH for October.

He's one of the SONS OF TEXAS and
ready to ride into your heart!

SDAB

COMING NEXT MONTH

#1042 A FATHER BETRAYED—Val Whisenand
Fabulous Fathers
Was Sami Adamson's child really his own? Clay Ellis didn't know—
but he refused to believe the woman he'd always loved would keep
him from the son he'd always wanted....

#1043 LONG LOST HUSBAND—Joleen Daniels
Andrea Ballanger thought her ex-husband, Travis Hunter, had been
killed in the line of duty. But when she learned Travis was very much
alive, she discovered her love was, too....

#1044 HARDHEADED WOMAN—Terry Essig
Divorce did wonders for Claire Martinson. Now that she had her
independence, she was determined to be a new woman. But how
was G. T. Greer going to convince her he'd fallen for the girl she'd
always been?

#1045 BACHELOR AT THE WEDDING—Sandra Steffen
Wedding Wager
When confirmed bachelor Kyle Harris caught the wedding garter,
he was surprisingly happy with the consequences. Now he just had
to convince would-be bride Clarissa Cohagan that *he* was the man
for *her*....

#1046 THE BABY WISH—Myrna Mackenzie
Gabriel Bonner was shocked when his pretty housekeeper,
Maureen O'Shay, asked him to father her child. Worse still, now
he was falling in love with her! What was a man who'd given up
on family life to do?

#1047 HOME TIES—Kara Larkin
Sterling, Montana, needed a doctor and Dr. Bryant Conover needed
a place to spend time with his son. He never expected to fall for
Deborah Pingree. Suddenly making house calls was *very* appealing....

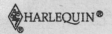 **HARLEQUIN®** 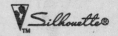 Silhouette®

The movie event of the season can be the reading event of the year!

Lights... The lights go on in October when CBS presents Harlequin/Silhouette Sunday Matinee Movies. These four movies are based on bestselling Harlequin and Silhouette novels.

Camera... As the cameras roll, be the first to read the original novels the movies are based on!

Action... Through this offer, you can have these books sent directly to you! Just fill in the order form below and you could be reading the books...before the movie!

48288-4	Treacherous Beauties by Cheryl Emerson		
	$3.99 U.S./$4.50 CAN.	☐
83305-9	Fantasy Man by Sharon Green		
	$3.99 U.S./$4.50 CAN.	☐
48289-2	A Change of Place by Tracy Sinclair		
	$3.99 U.S./$4.50CAN.	☐
83306-7	Another Woman by Margot Dalton		
	$3.99 U.S./$4.50 CAN.	☐

TOTAL AMOUNT	$
POSTAGE & HANDLING	$
($1.00 for one book, 50¢ for each additional)	
APPLICABLE TAXES*	$_____
<u>**TOTAL PAYABLE**</u>	$_____
(check or money order—please do not send cash)	

To order, complete this form and send it, along with a check or money order for the total above, payable to Harlequin Books, to: **In the U.S.:** 3010 Walden Avenue, P.O. Box 9047, Buffalo, NY 14269-9047; **In Canada:** P.O. Box 613, Fort Erie, Ontario, L2A 5X3.

Name: _____

Address: _____ City: _____

State/Prov.: _____ Zip/Postal Code: _____

*New York residents remit applicable sales taxes.
 Canadian residents remit applicable GST and provincial taxes.

CBSPR

"HOORAY FOR HOLLYWOOD" SWEEPSTAKES

HERE'S HOW THE SWEEPSTAKES WORKS

OFFICIAL RULES — NO PURCHASE NECESSARY

To enter, complete an Official Entry Form or hand print on a 3" x 5" card the words "HOORAY FOR HOLLYWOOD", your name and address and mail your entry in the pre-addressed envelope (if provided) or to: "Hooray for Hollywood" Sweepstakes, P.O. Box 9076, Buffalo, NY 14269-9076 or "Hooray for Hollywood" Sweepstakes, P.O. Box 637, Fort Erie, Ontario L2A 5X3. Entries must be sent via First Class Mail and be received no later than 12/31/94. No liability is assumed for lost, late or misdirected mail.

Winners will be selected in random drawings to be conducted no later than January 31, 1995 from all eligible entries received.

Grand Prize: A 7-day/6-night trip for 2 to Los Angeles, CA including round trip air transportation from commercial airport nearest winner's residence, accommodations at the Regent Beverly Wilshire Hotel, free rental car, and $1,000 spending money. (Approximate prize value which will vary dependent upon winner's residence: $5,400.00 U.S.); 500 Second Prizes: A pair of "Hollywood Star" sunglasses (prize value: $9.95 U.S. each). Winner selection is under the supervision of D.L. Blair, Inc., an independent judging organization, whose decisions are final. Grand Prize travelers must sign and return a release of liability prior to traveling. Trip must be taken by 2/1/96 and is subject to airline schedules and accommodations availability.

Sweepstakes offer is open to residents of the U.S. (except Puerto Rico) and Canada who are 18 years of age or older, except employees and immediate family members of Harlequin Enterprises, Ltd., its affiliates, subsidiaries, and all agencies, entities or persons connected with the use, marketing or conduct of this sweepstakes. All federal, state, provincial, municipal and local laws apply. Offer void wherever prohibited by law. Taxes and/or duties are the sole responsibility of the winners. Any litigation within the province of Quebec respecting the conduct and awarding of prizes may be submitted to the Regie des loteries et courses du Quebec. All prizes will be awarded; winners will be notified by mail. No substitution of prizes are permitted. Odds of winning are dependent upon the number of eligible entries received.

Potential grand prize winner must sign and return an Affidavit of Eligibility within 30 days of notification. In the event of non-compliance within this time period, prize may be awarded to an alternate winner. Prize notification returned as undeliverable may result in the awarding of prize to an alternate winner. By acceptance of their prize, winners consent to use of their names, photographs, or likenesses for purpose of advertising, trade and promotion on behalf of Harlequin Enterprises, Ltd., without further compensation unless prohibited by law. A Canadian winner must correctly answer an arithmetical skill-testing question in order to be awarded the prize.

For a list of winners (available after 2/28/95), send a separate stamped, self-addressed envelope to: Hooray for Hollywood Sweepstakes 3252 Winners, P.O. Box 4200, Blair, NE 68009.

CBSRLS

OFFICIAL ENTRY COUPON

"Hooray for Hollywood"
SWEEPSTAKES!

Yes, I'd love to win the Grand Prize — a vacation in Hollywood —
or one of 500 pairs of "sunglasses of the stars"! Please enter me
in the sweepstakes!

This entry must be received by December 31, 1994.
Winners will be notified by January 31, 1995.

Name _____

Address _____ Apt. _____

City _____

State/Prov. _____ Zip/Postal Code _____

Daytime phone number _____
(area code)

Mail all entries to: Hooray for Hollywood Sweepstakes,
P.O. Box 9076, Buffalo, NY 14269-9076.
In Canada, mail to: Hooray for Hollywood Sweepstakes,
P.O. Box 637, Fort Erie, ON L2A 5X3.

KCH

OFFICIAL ENTRY COUPON

"Hooray for Hollywood"
SWEEPSTAKES!

Yes, I'd love to win the Grand Prize — a vacation in Hollywood —
or one of 500 pairs of "sunglasses of the stars"! Please enter me
in the sweepstakes!

This entry must be received by December 31, 1994.
Winners will be notified by January 31, 1995.

Name _____

Address _____ Apt. _____

City _____

State/Prov. _____ Zip/Postal Code _____

Daytime phone number _____
(area code)

Mail all entries to: Hooray for Hollywood Sweepstakes,
P.O. Box 9076, Buffalo, NY 14269-9076.
In Canada, mail to: Hooray for Hollywood Sweepstakes,
P.O. Box 637, Fort Erie, ON L2A 5X3.

KCH